He hurried into his mom's closet and fumbled with the shoe box, reaching inside without looking, and removed the baseball. He held it up in the thick beam of late-afternoon light streaming through the window. The skin was smooth and yellowing with age; the seams had faded from red to almost pink. The writing was bold and dark, written in black Sharpie, but the signature was a meaningless squiggle.

Ryder turned the ball in his hand. He'd never thought about his father really, never allowed himself to. But now, now they needed to find him—to save her.

# ALSO BY TIM GREEN

# LOST BOY

## TIM GREEN

**HARPER**

*An Imprint of HarperCollinsPublishers*

Library of Congress Cataloging-in-Publication Data
Green, Tim, date
  Lost boy / by Tim Green. — First edition.
    pages cm
  Summary: After a near-fatal car accident, twelve-year-old Ryder's mother needs an
operation they cannot afford, and while a new friend tries to raise funds, Ryder travels
with a grouchy, disabled neighbor from Yankee Stadium to Turner Field, seeking the
Major League Baseball player who might be Ryder's father.
  ISBN 978-0-06-231709-4 (pbk.)
  [1. Mothers and sons—Fiction. 2. Fathers and sons—Fiction. 3. Identity—Fiction.
4. People with disabilities—Fiction. 5. Fund-raising—Fiction. 6. Baseball—Fiction.
7. Traffic accidents—Fiction.] I. Title.
PZ7.G826357Los 2015                                                    2014022682
[Fic]—dc23                                                                    CIP
                                                                              AC

Typography by Megan Stitt
17 18 19 20  OPM  10 9 8 7 6 5 4 3
❖
First paperback edition, 2016

# 1

Ryder smashed a ball over the fence and tried not to smile.

He jogged the bases while his teammates whistled, cat-called, or clapped, depending on the kind of person they were and which side they'd bet on. His team's best pitcher, Ben Salisbury, had said he'd strike Ryder out with four pitches. Ryder knocked it out on the second. Only the kids who went to Dalton School with Salisbury bet on him, and they did it out of loyalty. Everyone knew Ryder had the best Little League batting average in Manhattan.

Practice ended. The fields in Central Park were booked solid, so the team could never run over its assigned time.

Salisbury spoke in a superior tone of voice. "Anyone can get lucky. No way can you do that again. Tomorrow, let's go double or nothing . . . unless you're *scared*."

Ryder squinted at him in the bright sunshine filtering through the metal backstop.

"That's *if* you can make it till Friday without my twenty bucks and still have enough money to pay for your lunch." Salisbury waggled his eyebrows at his buddies and they all laughed.

Ryder shrugged without a word, pulled his coat on over his baseball uniform, and walked away. Some of his teammates were more upset about it than he was, and they cried foul. There was some pushing and shoving, but Ryder's eyes were already on his mom, and he marched toward her, not wanting her to have to be on her feet any longer than she needed. His mom cleaned the Pierre Hotel every day of the week—even today, Sunday—and he knew she never sat down. He'd heard the story about Mrs. Cruz, who sat down on the edge of a bathtub, got caught, and was fired. And his mom needed this job.

Jason Anton caught up to him just as Ryder's mom gave him a kiss on the cheek and a quick hug.

"Hi, Ms. Shoesmith." Jason actually tipped his cap to Ryder's mom. He was a private school kid too, Allen Stevenson School. Almost everyone on this select league team besides Ryder was.

"Call me Ruby, Jason. You're making me feel old." Ryder's mom was anything but old. She got mistaken for a college student all the time, and Ryder for her younger brother instead of her son.

"Okay, I'll try. Hey, man." Jason chucked Ryder's shoulder and spoke low. "You shouldn't have let him off like that. What a jerk.

"You should've seen him, Ms. Shoesmith. Ryder knocked a home run on Salisbury's second pitch and the bet was twenty dollars that he'd strike him out in four." Jason announced this with pride, but stopped smiling when he saw Ryder's mom frown.

2

"I didn't take it, Mom." Ryder shook his head at Jason and mouthed for him to shut up.

"Anyway, Ryder," Jason said, "Friday night there's this sleepover at the museum. It's an Egyptian party. Everyone gets wrapped up in toilet paper and there's magicians and snakes and all these contests. It's super fun and my mom said I could bring a guest, so . . . wanna come?"

Ryder didn't even look at his mom because he knew her reaction. "Oh, man, I wish I could. Sorry, Jason, but thanks a lot."

Jason's face dropped and he stopped walking. "You sure?"

"Naw, we got all this stuff planned for Friday, but thanks, Jason." Ryder turned to go.

"Hey," Jason said. "I'm gonna keep asking you, you know."

"Thanks," Ryder said.

"You do that, Jason. You're a very nice boy." Ryder's mom flashed a smile full of perfect white teeth, which outshined even the sun because of her tan skin and crow-black hair.

Ryder tugged her along without looking back, then jammed his hands deep in his coat pockets as they walked silently through the park. Tiny buds exploded lime green from the tips of many tree branches. Other branches bore only heavy purple pods, ready, but waiting for the real spring, not just a sunny day. Ryder smelled roasted chestnuts from some unseen vendor, probably out on Central Park West. He had never eaten one, but he loved the warm, rich smell of them.

His mom cleared her throat to get his attention. Ryder rolled his eyes and braced himself, because he already knew what was coming.

## 2

"Why do you always do that?" Her voice was soft, like her skin, like her full, dark hair.

"Do what?" Ryder knew she wouldn't like his reply, but couldn't help himself from playing dumb.

"Well, you know. We've had this discussion before."

"Let's not have it again," he said.

"I just *don't* want you to be . . ."

"What?" He flashed his eyes at her, daring her to say it.

She pressed her lips tight, then spoke. "A mama's boy, Ryder."

"Well, I am, so there." To tease her, he put a thumb in his mouth and began sucking on it.

"Oh, you!" She gave him a playful shove and he grabbed her, wrestling around and tickling her, right up underneath the arms of her bright yellow puffy coat until she screamed for him to stop. "Please!"

He did stop, and she tackled him, driving him off the sidewalk and onto the thin, muddy grass.

"You're crazy!" he shouted, laughing even though the mud soaked through the seat of his pants. "Help! My mother's lost her mind!"

She tickled him now, and he got her too, until they both laughed so hard they had tears in their eyes and they lay back together looking at the bright blue sky. Clouds thick and fat as whipped cream crept toward Long Island.

"Soon, you're not gonna stand a chance," he said.

"I know. You're growing up."

Part of Ryder liked the sound of that, but there was also something scary about it. He liked being friends with his mom and suspected growing up would change that. Like her pushing him to hang out with other kids. He didn't *want* to hang out with other kids. He was happy by himself, with a book, or with her.

She sighed. "He's so nice, that Jason."

"You can't let it go, can you?" He punched a fist into his baseball mitt. "Friday night is our movie night."

"It doesn't *have* to be. That's what I'm telling you."

"Why? You want to go out on a date?" He knew she got asked out all the time. He'd seen men stop cold on the street, even heard them suggest dinner sometime.

She slapped him lightly on the head. "I want you to be a boy. Boys hang out with their friends."

"It's hard to have friends when you don't even have a phone." He wanted to get her off the subject, and he knew it riled her when he complained about not having a phone.

She sighed. "Well, one day, you'll be a doctor and able to

afford cell phones for everyone. . . . I clean toilets."

Ryder's jacket felt suddenly tight and the ground cold and wet. He hated when she talked like that, hated that she cleaned other people's messes for a living. His voice got hard. "Yeah. One day."

He got up and so did she, the magic broken. They weren't friends anymore, they were a typical mom and kid, mad about things they didn't see eye to eye on. They started to walk, winding their way through the park along the familiar route that led from the baseball fields to a rough and run-down part of the city where they lived. What she said about cleaning toilets still bothered him, and he wanted to swing back. He took his time, searching for a plan of attack.

Finally, he had it. He cleared his throat and, to get her full attention, he held up the hand with the glove on it. "One day, I'll play in the majors and I'm gonna buy you a penthouse on Fifth Avenue."

He knew she hated the Upper East Side because that's where the real snobs lived—Trump, Bloomberg, the Hiltons. And the only thing she hated worse than anything old, loud, or excessively wealthy was a professional athlete. When the Mets signed Johan Santana to a $137 million contract and he showed her the sports page at the breakfast table, she snatched it from him, crumpled the paper, and jammed it in the trash.

"Focus on school." She had glared at him. "Those people aren't the ones you need to look up to. Look at A-Rod. It's a bad business, that sports. I don't care how much money there is in it."

Ryder shrugged to himself, remembering her words to him as she dragged him now along the sidewalk toward the

6

corner where they crossed 110th Street. The sirens on the street matched his mood—angry, desperate. Ryder wanted to break free from her grip. He was nearly as tall and as strong as she was now, and it didn't suit him to be manhandled by a tiny woman who looked like his sister. All he needed was a reason to fight back and tear himself free.

The sirens and blaring fire truck horns gave him a sense of urgency and strength. He stopped in his tracks.

She turned and glared, her feet just at the edge of the curb. "What are you doing?"

"I'm going back to the field. Play some catch with my 'friends.' You want me to have friends, right?" He removed her hand. "And I need the work if I'm going to be a pro."

"You're talking nonsense." She grabbed his arm again by the coat sleeve.

The noise of emergency vehicles grew so loud, it was deafening.

"No, I'm *not*." He snatched his arm free from her grip.

She stumbled backward off the curb, and tripped out into the street and in front of a roaring truck. He saw a blur, that's all, a blur. He opened his mouth to scream, but nothing came out.

She was just gone, and time floated like a dying balloon in a warm, empty room.

The truck that struck her swerved and ran the red light, crashing into the slow-moving stream of traffic and one of the fire trucks racing by. Tires shrieked. Metal smashed into metal, crunching human parts like chicken bones in the mouth of a pit bull.

3

"Mom?" Ryder whispered, in shock. He stood, blinking, his jaw hanging slack. He staggered, a zombie with feet dragging, arms crooked and swinging without rhythm. One of the vehicles in the pileup was a fire rescue truck, and in the corner of his mind something said that had to be a good thing.

A crowd quickly gathered, but they let him through. On the street in a dark puddle of yesterday's rain his mother lay looking at the sky.

"Oh, Lord. Don't you take her home, Lord," an older lady cried.

Ryder looked back to where the words had come from. An old lady in a gray wool cap that matched her long shabby coat poked her tongue out from the gap in her teeth in a grimace of pain. He wanted to tell her that everyone knew his mother was beautiful and—in his fog—that seemed an important thing to say, but his own tongue had no feeling.

A groan drew his attention back to his mother. The sound came from a fireman with the name "Raymer" sewn into his jacket. There were two firemen, and they knelt on either side of her, Raymer touching her neck, the other—whose coat said "McDonald"—with a hand on her bright yellow down coat and an ear to her lips. She lay still with her arms straight out and her long legs crooked and crossed at the ankles in their tight jeans. She'd been knocked right out of her Timberland boots. Ryder saw one lying crooked under a truck tire, yellow orange and new and unlaced the way she liked.

Her head lay in a glossy halo of silky black hair. Her enormous dark eyes stared wide and empty.

The fireman named Raymer removed his fingers from her neck and looked at his partner.

4

"Get the AED, Derek!" Doyle McDonald screamed before blowing into Ryder's mother's mouth and starting chest pumps, up and down, back and forth. Muscles jumped beneath the skin in his arms. It was a crazy dance that didn't end until the other fireman returned with a white plastic box and a pair of scissors.

"Mom?" Ryder repeated, a little louder now. Panic boiled over in Ryder's brain. He began to cry, knowing he'd caused it, desperate to take it back. Willing her to get up. If she did, she could drag him up and down the street all day and he'd never pull away.

Derek Raymer unzipped the jacket, then cut her black sweater up the middle and it fell away, baring Ryder's mother's honey-colored skin and her ribs to the cold sunshine and the crowd of strangers. It didn't seem to matter. Doyle already had two hand-sized paddles he'd removed from the box. The wires stretched across Ryder's mother and Doyle held the paddles up on either side of her chest, one high, one low.

"Everyone clear!" Doyle shouted.

Derek held his arms out and gave a nod. "Clear."

Doyle pressed the paddles into her chest. Her neck arched and her body went rigid. The shock ended. Doyle removed the paddles and looked at his partner. Derek felt her neck and shook his head.

Ryder choked and sobbed. "Mom!"

"Again!" Doyle bellowed. "Clear!"

"Clear," Derek said.

Doyle shocked her again. Derek felt her neck.

"Got something."

Even in his fog, Ryder felt his own heart clench with hope. Doyle was blowing air into her lungs again and did so until Derek returned, this time with an oxygen mask. A siren screamed as an ambulance screeched to a stop on the street. Two EMTs appeared. Doyle shouted for a stretcher. The men barked at each other, urgent and direct. Their words were a scramble.

"Internal bleeding."

"Heart stopped."

"Breathing."

"Irregular."

"Hurry."

"Go."

They loaded her in. Ryder wandered close, but was lost, speechless among all the chaos. Doyle stood with one hand on the ambulance door and looked back. "Anyone with her?"

Everyone took a half step back except Ryder. He still couldn't speak, but his hand came partway up and Doyle found his eyes.

"Come on."

Ryder took the fireman's hand and was packed into the back of the ambulance like a suitcase, tucked into the corner while Doyle and the heavy EMT with a goatee slammed the doors shut and bent to work over his mother. Ryder hooked his fingers under the lip of the seat with one hand; on his other hand he still wore the baseball mitt. He bumped along and leaned into the turns to keep from falling over. It wasn't far to the hospital and when they stopped, the doors flew open and people in pale blue scrubs and masks and caps reached for his mother as the EMT and the fireman slid the gurney out to them.

In a flurry, she was gone. The EMT climbed down and disappeared around the front of the ambulance. The fireman straightened and his thinning brown hair brushed the ceiling. His face was wide and red and made for smiling, even though much of his mouth was hidden by a mustache big as a push broom. He turned to Ryder with glistening eyes and he sniffed and wiped them on his sleeve.

"Okay, bud. Let's get you inside and get someone to take care of you."

Ryder sat still until the fireman named Doyle took his arm. Ryder stood up and Doyle helped him down from the ambulance. Doyle put a hand on his shoulder and they walked inside together. They stopped in front of a desk where an orange-haired woman behind the counter chewed gum. A scary green-and-yellow dragon tattoo curled around the side of her neck, but her smile was cheerful.

"Hey, little man. Do you have a dad?"

Ryder opened his mouth to answer that question, but it wasn't an easy one to answer under the best of circumstances, so nothing came out.

Doyle kept his hand on Ryder's shoulder and leaned over to study the confusion on his face. "Is there anyone else we should call? Does your mom have a boyfriend? Maybe you got a grandma or an aunt or a friend?"

Now Ryder's eyes began to water, so he clamped his lip between his teeth and shook his head before he gave the answer that was so big and so awful it crushed him.

"No. We got no one."

# 5

"What's your name, hon?" the lady behind the desk asked.

"Ryder. Ryder Strong."

"How about your mom's name?" she asked.

"Ruby."

"Ruby Strong?"

"No, her last name is Shoesmith. Ruby Alice Shoesmith."

"But you said you don't have a father? Is she your real mom?" The woman was trying to stay patient. "Who can we call to come get you?"

"I'm Doyle McDonald," the firefighter interrupted. "Look, he's upset." Doyle gave the lady behind the counter a serious look and pointed to the FDNY patch on his sleeve. "I got him."

The lady stopped chewing her gum. "We're also gonna need insurance information from someone."

"Let me settle him down and find out who else there is and

I'll get back to you." Doyle offered a smile of strong white teeth beneath the bushy mustache. "Promise."

"Sure," the lady said, nodding. Ryder wasn't surprised that the lady accepted the promise of a fireman like a gold coin. Firemen were heroes. Everyone knew that.

"Who can we talk to about his mom? How she's doing?" Doyle asked.

"Someone will be out soon. You can have a seat over there to wait." The lady pointed to a waiting room before she returned to her computer.

"Okay. Thanks." Doyle nodded and steered Ryder to a plastic-covered chair bound together with others in a long row against the wall. They sat down in the two seats that were closest to the double doors where Ryder's mom had gone in.

Ryder couldn't hold still. "I have to see her. I *have* to."

Doyle looked sympathetically at Ryder's tears. He studied the reception desks for less than a minute before he mashed a finger to his lips, stood, and silently waved Ryder toward the double doors, which hissed open automatically. Inside the doors was a hive of activity—a series of hallways stuffed with medical equipment, patients on gurneys, and nurses and doctors hurrying to and fro.

Doyle stopped the first nurse he saw. "I need to see the female trauma who just came in. I was at the scene."

The nurse took a quick look at his uniform, hesitated when she saw Ryder, but pointed down the hall anyway. "You better hurry, they've got her in EOR 3 and they're gonna open her up."

Doyle nodded, took Ryder by the arm, and headed in the

direction of the operating room.

They passed a room guarded by two policemen. Inside, a young man with a bandana around his head screamed in pain while a handful of hospital people tried to hold him down. His lower leg flopped around on its own like a fish and blood was everywhere. Ryder swallowed and felt Doyle's tug.

They stopped outside the operating room and its double doors. Ryder was tall for his age, but the windows didn't let him see in. Doyle studied whatever was going on. His tan face lost some color and his grip tightened on Ryder's arm. He tugged Ryder aside as a young woman in scrubs emerged with blood spatters on her pale blue mask and hat.

"How is she?" Doyle asked.

The doctor looked at Ryder. "He can't be here."

"I know," Doyle said. "I got him, though."

"You should not be here, either," she said.

Doyle pointed to the firefighter patch on his sleeve, which everyone knew was as good as a key to the city. "How is she?"

The doctor shook her head and started off down the hall. "Not good."

"Maybe we should wait outside," Doyle said. "You're not going to be able to see her."

"What about over there." Ryder pointed to two chairs across the hall. "So we're closer."

Doyle looked around. "Yeah, okay. Good."

They sat down and Ryder tried to listen through the doors. All he heard was muffled voices. Once in a while there would be the muted bark of an order. The terror weighed on Ryder, making it hard to breathe. His brain spun like a wobbly top.

When a nurse hurried out, they stood up and heard a lot of noise from inside. It didn't sound good. The nurse didn't pause, but disappeared, only to come rushing back with someone else.

Ryder's heart never left his throat. He could feel it beating there, choking him, but he didn't move. It might have been twenty minutes or twenty hours. He had no idea, only the vague sense that he had to use the bathroom. Hunger never rose its head. His stomach was closed for business. Doyle worked silently on an iPhone, but stayed beside him, solid as stone.

Finally, the doors burst open and a handful of doctors and nurses emerged, faces drawn tight, scrubs spattered with his mother's blood. He knew by the way they undid their masks and whisked off their caps that it was over. He and Doyle stood at the same moment. Their eyes went from him to Doyle.

Doyle choked out the words. "How is she?"

Everyone turned to the boss, a small woman doctor.

She cast a disapproving look at Doyle, then her eyes softened when she saw Ryder and she took a deep breath.

6

"She is alive," the doctor said in a lilting Indian accent.

Doyle exhaled in a burst of joy.

Ryder felt his insides relax. Warmth flooded his entire body.

When he realized the doctor's face didn't match her words, though, everything cramped up again. He looked up at Doyle, who saw it too, and frowned at the doctor.

"What's wrong?" Doyle asked.

"Who are you?" The doctor's syrupy accent rolled the *r*'s softly off her tongue, the *o*'s sounding like a song. "You should not even be in here."

The other doctors and nurses melted away, leaving just the three of them standing there.

Doyle put a protective hand on Ryder's neck. "I'm a fireman, but I'm a close family friend. I'm all they've got. This is her son."

Ryder only nodded, not happy about lying, but wanting more information about his mom.

The doctor took a deep breath. "I have another surgery I need to do now. She's alive, but she's very sick."

"Like, it'll be a long road?" Doyle asked.

The doctor stared at him hard, then bit into her lower lip and shook her head. "A short road . . . Her heart is very damaged and things are not working right. I think she will need a new valve, maybe two valves. Her heart cannot continue like this."

"Well." Doyle brightened. "You guys do that all the time, right? Valves?"

The doctor shook her head. "It can be done, but this is a very difficult area."

The doctor gave a worried look at Ryder and lowered her voice. "It is very costly."

"What about insurance or something?" Doyle asked.

"Even if she has insurance, they don't pay for everything. It's very complicated. The hospital administrator can explain more."

"Well, I can pay for it." Doyle stuck out his chest. "How much is it?"

"Something like this?" The doctor's eyes didn't waver. "It would be two hundred thousand dollars, at least."

"Two . . ." Doyle swallowed and his hand slipped off of Ryder's neck. "What if they don't have that kind of money?"

"These are not my decisions." The doctor shook her head. "I'm very sorry."

"How long do I . . . we have? To get the money?"

"She cannot go very long as she is. Three, maybe four weeks. Now, I must go."

"Can I see her?" Ryder asked.

"She's in recovery, then they'll move her to ICU. You can see her there, but it will be at least another two or three hours before you can go in."

"Can she talk?" Doyle asked.

"She will be in pain, so she will be medicated. She also has a broken femur, three broken ribs, and a ruptured spleen." The doctor spoke softly. "She might not recognize you. I'm sorry, but she is lucky just to be alive."

Ryder watched her walk away.

Doyle cleared his throat. "Okay, well. You never know what can happen, and she's okay for now, right? You gotta look at the positives. Come on, kid. Let me get you a soda or something, and maybe we can figure out what we're gonna do."

Ryder followed, his mind still churning over everything that had happened and what he'd just heard. It was like a vat of messy soup. There was still a kind of buzzing in his ears and a fuzziness around the edges of his vision. Doyle led him back through the emergency waiting room, then outside before reentering the hospital through the main doors. They found the cafeteria. It smelled of cleaning compounds and cheap food. Doyle bought a coffee for himself and a Coke for Ryder. They sat down at a small round table in the corner.

"You want to take your coat off?" Doyle asked.

Ryder shrugged. He didn't care if it was off or on.

"Now, listen, buddy. There's gotta be *someone* you and your mom know. If you don't have family, you must have had a

20

babysitter growing up, or someone who watches you when your mom has to go out or something? Think, buddy."

Ryder shook his head. "Just Mr. Starr, but hardly ever."

"Mr. Starr. Great. See? He's someone."

Ryder shook his head. "He can't do anything and he doesn't have a phone."

"You don't need a phone. How do you know him?"

"He lives across the hall from our apartment."

"Perfect. See? A neighbor across the hall who's watched you before. That'll work. That way you don't have to go into a foster care home or something while this all gets sorted out. You don't want to go into a home. Trust me."

It hit Ryder like a tidal wave, suddenly and with tremendous force.

He burst into tears and a moan of terrible pain escaped his throat as he began to sob.

"Hey, hey. Come on, buddy." Doyle slid his chair over and put an arm around Ryder's shoulders. "I don't know what to say here. . . . I mean, I got no kids or anything. Don't worry, I guess. It's gonna be okay."

"No! It's not!" Ryder choked on his words. He could barely breathe.

"My mom is gonna *die*!"

Doyle held on to him awkwardly, and after a while, Ryder had no more tears. He sniffed and Doyle seemed relieved to let him go. Doyle handed him some napkins to clean his face. Ryder shook his head and stood up, not caring about the looks from the other people in the cafeteria.

"Let's go to your place." Doyle spoke in a gentle voice that didn't match his big, bulky frame. "You can drop off your base-ball glove and get out of that uniform, and we can talk to Mr. Starr. Sound good? We got time. We can go there and then come back and see your mom. Okay?"

"Okay." As Doyle steered him outside, Ryder looked down at the baseball mitt he'd forgotten was still on his hand.

Doyle hailed a cab, which took them to where Ryder and his mom lived, a crumbling five-story brick building where they shared a one-bedroom apartment. Spray paint soiled the concrete front steps. An old yellow door showed brown rust around the edges, and the round handle sagged uselessly. The other door was missing completely.

Ryder felt embarrassed by the shabby entrance. From the darkened hallway came the sounds of shouting and the screams of a baby.

"Be careful of the railing." Ryder put a hand on the old thing, carved from wood decades ago, and wiggled it as proof that it wasn't to be trusted in the least to do its job.

They climbed the darkened stairway, up all five flights. They heard more shouting and crying and loud music thumping behind doors. Each floor had its own smell, none of them good, even the third where a family from Pakistan cooked exotic meat with spices you'd think might be nice, but they were so rich they nearly made Ryder's empty stomach heave. Finally, they reached the top landing where they turned right and went to the very end of the hall before Ryder fished the key from his jacket pocket. He kept it tied to his belt on a New York Giants lanyard. He jiggled the key into the lock, letting them into the tiny apartment that was as pleasant a refuge in such a place as to make it almost magical.

Ryder's mom kept everything neat and clean, and several glowing floor lamps filled the apartment with a yellow-orange warmth that could almost be felt. The scent of homey spices like cloves, dried basil, and cinnamon from the galley kitchen greeted them at the door. The smells made him think of her. The sight of her pale blue bunny slippers waiting hopelessly on the mat just inside the door made him choke on a fist-sized lump in his throat.

"Nice little place." Doyle peered into the living room with its single curtained window, an old leather love seat, a carved golden oak table with matching high-backed chairs, and shelves crammed with musty books from floor to ceiling. At the closer edge of the room was an overstuffed chair with a blue-and-white decorative porcelain reading lamp on a narrow table beside it. "She reads a lot, huh?"

Ryder nodded wordlessly.

Doyle pointed to a shelf in the corner, the only one that wasn't packed with books. Nearly a dozen trophies stood glinting with pride. "Yours?"

Ryder nodded again. "Yeah," he mumbled.

"Okay. Nice. You gonna change?"

Ryder shrugged and went into the only bedroom. He and his mom each had their own twin bed against opposite walls. He tried to ignore all the normal things around the room as he tossed his glove in the closet, stripped down, and pulled on jeans and a hoodie. He didn't want any reminders of their normal life. He was already desperately hungry for it. He couldn't believe this was happening—how stupid he felt for being so angry at his mom. Even the saddest or most irritating moments in his life before now seemed sweet in comparison to what was going on. His "now" was no place to be, and he gave himself a little curse for taking everything for granted.

So, he ignored the split personality of the room. Her side was painted pale pink with tiny purple flowers on the wall and lace pillows on her bed. On the nightstand was a decorative antique lamp. On his side, the walls were off-white and sported his own team pictures amid posters of Derek Jeter, A-Rod, and Mickey Mantle as a sign of respect for the team's great tradition.

The cover on his bed and the pillow were both speckled with the Yankees logo. Baseball trophies of many sizes and shapes crowded the top of his dresser.

He shook his head and kept his eyes on the floor, returning to the living room the instant he was dressed.

Doyle replaced the book he'd been studying to its empty spot on the shelf. "So, where's this Starr guy?"

"Okay. He's across the hall." Ryder led Doyle back out into the hall and threw the bolt so the door to his apartment wouldn't close behind them. He knocked on the next door over and waited.

"Maybe he's not home?" Doyle stroked his mustache.

Ryder shook his head and found his voice. "No. He's always home."

"Always?"

"You'll see." Ryder knocked again.

The screech from within was muffled, but clearly unwelcoming. "*Who* is it?"

Ryder put his mouth to the crack and shouted. "Mr. Starr? It's Ryder."

There was some muted thumping, then silence for several minutes.

"I think he's coming," Ryder said.

"You do?"

Ryder nodded because he now heard the faint high-pitched whisper of a motor that slowly approached from the other side of the door. There was a bump against the door and some indistinct cursing from within before the locks rattled over and over again.

Finally the rattling stopped and the motor sound backed up

before Mr. Starr shouted, "Well? Come in!"

Ryder grabbed the knob, turned it, and swung open the door. Doyle made a small sound of surprise at the sight of Mr. Starr.

Mr. Starr glared at them from where he sat rigid and upright in his wheelchair, his big dark eyes made bigger yet by the glasses he wore. His face was frozen in a mask of discomfort, drawn down at the corners of his mouth and eyes, his head stuck in an immovable tilt that suggested either disgust or retreat. The lopsided skull beneath his pale scalp sprouted thin black strands that looked more like damp thread than hair, and both his arms seemed stuck at uncomfortable angles. One wrist was more crooked than the other.

"It's not polite to stare." Mr. Starr's lips had all the flexibility in the world. "Even if your brain works slow. I've found most firemen have slow brains. It's not a career for the quick-witted, running into burning buildings. . . ."

Ryder shifted uncomfortably because there was no tone of joking in Mr. Starr's voice. "Mr. Starr, my mom had an accident."

"Well, she's a careless young woman, what do you expect?"

"Hey." Doyle put a hand on Ryder's shoulder. "I think you can be nice to Ryder. Aren't you a friend?"

"Friends?" Mr. Starr glared, unblinking. "I am relied upon in emergencies only. I don't have friends."

"She was hit by a truck." Doyle sounded bitter and offended. "She's in the hospital."

"What truck? *Your* truck?" Mr. Starr's eyes burned with mean delight when Doyle winced.

"No," Doyle said, "not my truck."

"But your truck had a hand in it." Mr. Starr struck the arm of his chair and kept talking. "Racing through the streets, blaring your horn, causing others to run down innocent people? I'd rather have fibrodysplasia ossificans progressiva. . . . Oh . . . I already do."

Mr. Starr stared and Doyle obviously didn't know what to say.

"Your truck?" Ryder couldn't help asking, and he suddenly wondered if that was why Doyle was being so nice.

Doyle's mustache quivered but nothing came out of his mouth for a moment before he said, "There was an accident. Look, can you watch him for a few days while we sort things out?"

"Can he stay in his apartment with the door open and I stay in mine—with the door not wide open but unlocked—until his mother gets better so that social services doesn't whisk him away to a foster home where he's beaten or neglected? Is that what you're asking?"

Doyle gritted his teeth. "Yes."

The mean look on Mr. Starr's face didn't change, but it never did. His eyes shifted to Ryder, and Ryder stared back, trying not to cry while he waited for an answer.

# 8

Ryder's mom always said that inside Mr. Starr's frozen and twisted body was a person who used to run and laugh and smile. She said that person didn't get to come out very much but that was because he was shackled in pain from his disease. That was the word she used, "shackled," and Ryder knew it meant bound by iron rings and chains. So he had learned to feel sorry for Mr. Starr because he couldn't imagine being in so much pain and—like his mom—he didn't let the mean words Mr. Starr often used hurt him at all. His mom said they were like bullets from a Nerf gun and that's how he should think of them.

When Ryder saw the way Mr. Starr's eyes looked at him through their bulging lenses, he already knew what the answer was going to be.

"Ryder is a good boy," Mr. Starr said. "If I could help him

or his mother by driving this infernal machine into the service elevator shaft, I'd consider it a bargain worthy of losing my soul to the devil himself."

Ryder looked up at Doyle and smiled for the first time since everything had happened. "That means yes."

"Yeah, I get that." Doyle was still sulky. "Firemen go up and down the service elevators all the time."

Ryder thought he could fix things when they were alone, and he could explain Mr. Starr to Doyle, then realized he should have done that *before* they knocked on the door.

"Can I be of further assistance to you?" Mr. Starr glared at Doyle again. "Would you like me to contact the mayor's office and advocate for an even better pension plan than you already have?"

"I'm trying to help, you know." Doyle glared right back.

"Yes," Mr. Starr said. "I do know."

"Social services can be rough," Doyle said. "Now I can tell the folks at the hospital that he's okay, that there's a neighbor who's a family friend who watches him all the time who he can stay with while . . . while she gets better. That's all I'm trying to do here."

"From your face and tone, her getting better seems to be in doubt, so you also better think about something long-term," Mr. Starr said. "If social services gets their way, *I* won't be here much longer either."

Doyle scratched his head and reached for the door, speaking as he closed it. "Thank you, Mr. Starr. It's been a real pleasure."

"The boy does have a father, you know," Mr. Starr said.

Doyle looked at Ryder.

"I don't have a father." Ryder cast his eyes at the floor. "I never saw him."

"But he *has* a father," Mr. Starr said.

"Who is he?" Doyle asked.

Mr. Starr shut his eyes for a moment, as if in thought.

Ryder drew a breath and held it. He had no idea what was coming.

## 9

"That, we don't know," Mr. Starr said. "Ruby never told me. The whole thing with Ryder was very . . . traumatic. I think that's why you're standing at the mouth of a monster's lair instead of on the doorstep of an aging grandparent or a cheerful aunt."

Ryder's heart went cold. He knew his mother talked like she had no family, but he never knew *he* was the cause. He looked up at Doyle, whose mouth sagged open. "You mean they abandoned her?"

"To the family Ruby once had," Mr. Starr said, "she doesn't exist, really. She even changed her last name to insure there'd never be a connection. And thus, the heroic neighbor. Me. But it's a temporary solution at best. So, if Ruby is as bad as the look on your face tells me she is, you'd do well to find the father . . . not the family. Now, please go. I have things to do."

"Come on." Doyle tugged the back of Ryder's shirt, drawing him into the hallway.

"Thanks, Mr. Starr." Ryder didn't know what else to say, and Mr. Starr said nothing in return as he motored up to the door and hooked it with a claw so he could swing it toward them.

The door clicked shut and they could hear the whir of the chair's motor as it took Mr. Starr back into the depths of his apartment.

"Wow." Doyle spoke in a low tone. "Sorry for that."

Ryder followed Doyle down the stairs. "My mom says his bark is much worse than his bite."

"Was that his bark? I feel like I just got bit."

Ryder frowned.

"Hey, don't worry. It'll all work out. This way I can honestly tell them you've got somebody to keep an eye on you, and you get to sleep in your own bed." Doyle stopped on the second-floor landing and looked around, sniffing at the warm smell of spices from the third floor and the stink from the second. "Is this place safe?"

"The fifth floor is the safest because no one wants to climb the stairs." Ryder repeated the assurances his mom had given him since he could remember.

"Yeah. Even crooks are lazy these days." Doyle started down again.

"You sound like Mr. Starr."

"I'm not *that* grumpy. Could you believe all that fireman stuff? If this building ever went up in flames he'd be kissing our boots."

They reached the bottom steps and walked out into the bright afternoon sunlight, where Ryder paused and his eyes met Doyle's.

"She was trying to get me to go home. We were fighting

and I told her I was going back to the park to play ball with friends. She pulled me, but I yanked away. Then . . . she stumbled into the street."

Doyle pressed his lips together tight, then said, "Things happen, Ryder. Trust me, I see them every day. It's got nothing to do with you."

"The school said Mr. Starr can't be my emergency contact because he's disabled and he doesn't have a phone."

"I get that." Doyle tugged on his arm and they began to walk up the street toward Frederick Douglass Boulevard. "The phone part. But sometimes the rules don't fit and you have to fudge them a little. Not break them, just fudge them."

Ryder nodded.

"Listen, I'm gonna make some calls. I've seen FDNY do some pretty gigantic fund-raisers. . . . Maybe we can raise some of the money needed for your mom's medical bills."

"Really?" Ryder looked up and his heart thumped wildly.

"Well. Wait. I mean, I can't promise two hundred thousand . . . but I'll try, Ryder. I will. I'll do everything I possibly can."

On Frederick Douglass Boulevard they got a cab and headed toward the hospital.

"I know you don't know your dad, Ryder," Doyle said, "but do you know anything about him? Anything that could give us a clue? Mr. Starr is right, a neighbor with health issues is not a permanent solution, and your mom could be in the hospital for a while."

Ryder thought for a few minutes. "I think he was a good baseball player. When I play I'm really good, and like if I hit a home run or snag a line drive, sometimes she'll say that's the

33

only part of me that came from my father."

"Like he was a college player, or a pro?"

Ryder shrugged. "She never said. Whenever I ask her what she means, she closes her mouth tight and shakes her head and that's it. But I think he might have been, because my mom keeps a baseball that I think he might have signed."

"Signed?"

"Like an autograph. I don't know." Ryder bit his lower lip. He knew it wasn't smart to talk to strangers, but this was a fireman, and also, something about Doyle made him seem like he wasn't a stranger at all. "She keeps it hidden in the back of her closet, in a shoe box, and I never told her I found it. It says: 'With Love for Ruby, My Gem.'"

"And what's the signature? Who signed it?"

Ryder shrugged. "I have no idea. It doesn't look like anything but some squiggles to me. You can't *read* it."

"Well, maybe we can get some more out of her . . . if she's up for it." Doyle turned his attention out the cab's window. The day had grown late and the traffic was thicker now. Headlights blinked on and taillights glowed red. While the earlier sunshine spoke of spring, winter reclaimed its ground, lowering the temperature in the shadows so that pedestrians turned up their collars and tugged down their hats.

Ryder looked down, staring at Doyle's boots. He wondered about firefighters' boots. He knew they sometimes collected donations in them, mostly one-dollar bills, and he wondered how many they would have to fill to make two hundred thousand dollars, and he worried that there might not be enough fire boots in all of New York City to save his mother.

# 10

When they got back to the hospital, his mother still wasn't out of the recovery room. Doyle took him back to the cafeteria and got a coffee for himself and a purple Gatorade for Ryder, even though he said he didn't want anything. They sat at a different table in a different corner. Doyle scrunched up his face and studied his iPhone.

Ryder sat in a daze and stared out a window at the brick wall of the building next to them. Maybe he should have listened to his mom and made friends. It wasn't that kids didn't like him, or that he didn't like them. He could think of nearly a dozen kids he talked to in school and a handful on his team he liked, like Jason, but he never really got to know any of them *well*. He had no one to talk to, no one to confide in, no one to share his anguish and to provide even a sliver of comfort. He sat mulling these things—wishing he could do them over again—until he realized Doyle was talking to him.

"What?" Ryder asked. "I'm sorry."

Doyle held up his iPhone. "I said that I've been tweeting about your mom and people really seem to be into helping. See? I've got forty-seven retweets for hashtag Save Ruby! And I just started."

Ryder didn't have an iPhone and neither did his mom, just plain old ten-dollar TracFones with the bare-minimum calling plan for emergencies only. He'd heard of tweeting and knew it was something rich and famous people did to voice their opinions and sell albums or theater tickets. It burned him not to know about Twitter or Instagram or any of that stuff the kids on his travel baseball team were always doing. Anger flared in his chest. Then he remembered the mean tone of the words he'd had with his mom in the minutes before she was hit. The idea that those might be the last words they exchanged flooded him with guilt.

"Is forty-seven a lot?" he asked.

"Well, I only have two hundred and five followers, so it's not a *lot*, but I think it shows that the people who do see it want to help, get it?"

"I think so." Ryder watched an old man set down two Styrofoam cups of coffee, spilling one of them onto his wife and sparking an argument. "Two hundred thousand is a lot, though."

"Yeah, but if I could get two hundred thousand tweets, and everybody just gave a dollar . . ." Doyle studied the iPhone screen and muttered to himself. "Maybe FDNY. That's what I need. If I can get the entire New York City Fire Department working on this, that would do it for sure." Doyle looked up, eyes sparkling. "Right?"

"I guess." Ryder tried not to get too excited, but Doyle McDonald's enthusiasm had already cast its spell.

Doyle began typing furiously. "Calling . . . all . . . FDNY members . . . 911 to save the life of . . . Wait." Doyle looked up. "Do you have any photos of your mom?"

Ryder shook his head. "At home, maybe."

"Ephotos? On an iPhone or an iPad anywhere."

"No."

"Hey, we can take one." Doyle stood up. "Let's go check. Maybe she's out of recovery. If I take a picture of her and post that . . ."

"Why?"

"People like pretty women. It could go viral. Come on." Doyle started across the cafeteria, leaving his coffee cup to stand alone at their table. Ryder grabbed his Gatorade and had to hustle to keep up.

They soon learned that his mom was out of recovery and had been moved into the intensive care unit, or ICU. A heavy nurse with curly red hair and small dark eyes stopped them at the desk.

"We're here to see Ruby Shoesmith. How is she?" Doyle asked.

"She's breathing on her own so she doesn't have a tube," the nurse said, "but her heart rate isn't what they'd like to see." The nurse nodded at Ryder. "Is he fourteen?"

"I'm—"

"Yes." Doyle cut him off. "He's her son. Just turned fourteen."

The nurse gave Doyle a doubtful look, but shrugged and let them go.

Except for the wires and the IV tube stuck into her arm, his mother looked like she did when he woke her from an afternoon nap, her lips full and peaceful with a small smile, her brow smooth above the long, dark lashes of her eyes, and her hair a soft swirl of black silk. Her color might have been off a bit, but that also could be the humming neon lights above the tilted-up bed. Other things beeped and hummed as well, monitors to tell whether or not her heart and brain were alive and kicking. Despite his worry, Ryder looked up and gave Doyle a proud nod as the fireman took out his iPhone to snap her picture.

"Can I talk to her?" He looked at the nurse who had been adjusting the monitors when they walked in.

The nurse nodded. "You can try. She's mumbled a little. Nothing I could understand. She's in and out of it. Her leg is broken and that's really painful, so we're giving her morphine."

Doyle held up the photo on his phone. "What do you think? She really is pretty, right?"

Ryder nodded and set down his Gatorade on the counter. Doyle returned to his tweeting.

Ryder moved close to his mom. Except for the hum and beep of the machines, it seemed impossible that she was even hurt, let alone in any danger. She looked *lovely* and peaceful. He reached out, wanting to touch her, but too afraid to really do it.

"Mom?" Ryder tried to fight back his tears, but the thought of losing her crushed his insides.

Suddenly she groaned and muttered something.

Her eyes fluttered open. She looked his way, but more

through him than at him. "Jimmy?"

"Mom, it's me, Ryder."

He felt Doyle at his side and the fireman put a hand on his shoulder. "What'd she say?"

"She said 'Jimmy.'"

"Who's Jimmy?" Doyle asked.

"There isn't anyone." It bothered Ryder that she hadn't recognized him. It scared him, too.

Doyle leaned close. "Ruby, I'm a friend. Is Jimmy Ryder's dad? Who's Ryder's father? We need to find Ryder's father. It's important."

"Father?" Her face clouded over and she turned her head away with a groan. "Not my father. No."

"*Ryder's* father? Who's *Ryder's* father?" Doyle spoke softly, but insistently.

She looked back at Doyle before shifting her blurred attention to Ryder. Her eyes filled with tears and she whispered, "Jimmy."

"It's me, Mom. It's Ryder." Tears spilled from his eyes and his face contorted with anguish.

"Don't tease, Jimmy Trent." His mother's smile faded into a scolding frown.

The monitor started to go crazy, beeping loudly.

"Oh, no. I'm getting the doctor." The nurse rushed past Ryder, then hurried out of the room.

His mother's eyes widened, then they closed.

11

In the flurry of activity, Ryder got swept to the side.

The bark and shout of orders was enough to unsettle him, and Ryder cried out and rushed back to his mother's bed.

The doctor glared over his shoulder. "Get that kid out of here!"

Doyle and a nurse grabbed Ryder and dragged him out. "Mom!" Ryder called, crying.

In the hallway, Doyle hugged him tight. "Shhh. Come on, buddy. She's gonna be okay. You gotta . . . think positive."

Ryder shook his head and sobbed, "I can't think anything!"

"Hey, hey. Shhh. Come on, now."

Ryder broke free and ran away from it all, down the hallway, through the doors, and into the stairwell. His feet slapped in a quick rhythm. Down he went, aware of the door being flung open above him and that the heavy thunk of steps was

Doyle in pursuit. Ryder reached the bottom and banged open the door. He dashed through the hospital lobby, winded from crying and running. He shoved his way through the exit.

Concrete benches crouched outside a small shadowed courtyard between the entrance and the sidewalk. Above, brown-painted metal awnings offered cover from only the most feeble weather. Ryder threw himself down on a bench and slouched with his hands jammed into his coat pockets against the cold. Vapor huffed from his mouth in great white puffs.

Scared and confused, he kept hearing his mother's voice in his head, calling out the name Jimmy Trent. Was that his father's name? He felt a sharp stab of pain, as if all the times he'd been upset about not having a father hit him at once. Fathers' night for his baseball team. Drawing a family tree in fourth grade. A teacher scolding him by asking if Ryder thought his father would approve of his behavior. There were hundreds of those moments. Spread out and alone, they were like paper cuts—annoying, but nothing to cry about. All together, it was a knife in his heart and it filled his eyes with more tears.

He sniffed and dabbed at his eyes, and after a few minutes, Doyle walked up and sat down next to him. They sat that way for a while, quiet and together as people passed them by, both coming and going.

Finally, Doyle spoke. "I've been looking for you."

Ryder shrugged.

"If you promise to wait right here," Doyle said, "I'll go check and see how she's doing. Okay?"

"Fine," Ryder said.

"Fine, you promise?"

He nodded. "I promise."

"Good." Doyle patted his leg and got up to go. "Right here."

Ryder suffered the entire time Doyle was gone and he could have kicked himself for not going along, but he promised he'd wait, so he did. Finally, the hefty fireman returned with a big grin. "Well, she's out of the woods. They won't be letting us in again tonight, though."

Ryder didn't respond, even though the flood of relief made him so dizzy that he tried to breathe deeply through his nose and let it out slow. They sat quietly for a while before Doyle's phone played a tune.

Doyle checked the new text that had come in. "Hey, Chief wants to see me. Wow, on a Sunday. Want to see the firehouse?"

"No." Ryder didn't look up.

"C'mon, kids love the firehouse. Big trucks. Chrome so bright it makes you blink."

"I'm not a kid," Ryder said.

"Okay, *young people* like the firehouse. You can slide down the pole. C'mon."

"There's not a pole," Ryder said.

"Honest to God, and you can go down it. Plus, I know for a fact that my partner—the guy you saw, Derek Raymer—has a big pot of chili like you never tasted. He won the blue ribbon at last year's Firefighters' Cookoff." Doyle stood and held out a hand, offering it to help Ryder up. "Come on. You'll meet the chief, not that he's anything but a slab-sided blowhard, but hey, he wears the white hat so . . ."

Ryder finally nodded and stood up. They took the subway to 125th Street, then walked to a brick building that was only about ten blocks from where Ryder lived. Two huge red doorways revealed the big trucks, resting like attack dogs with their chrome shiny enough for Ryder to see his bulging face in every spot. Men in dark blue pants and light blue shirts worked at various duties around the garage. They all cast wary looks at Doyle, as if they knew what had happened. There really was a shiny brass pole that disappeared through a hole in the ceiling.

"C'mon, kid. You can do that later. First, the chief." Doyle nudged his shoulder and Ryder followed the fireman into the station, where he got a whiff of chili before they climbed up two flights of stairs.

The office looked like any office Ryder had ever seen, crowded with papers and desks. Since it was Sunday, the desks in the gloomy space were empty, but in the far corner, light spilled from a single office.

"This is Battalion," Doyle explained. "Not every station is this big. We got lucky. We get to have the bosses right over our heads breathing down our necks every doggone minute."

They wound their way through the desks and walked right into the office with the lights.

"Hey, Chief." Doyle sat right down and crossed his legs, directing Ryder to the chair beside him with a nod of his head.

The chief looked up from some papers and glared at Doyle. "What are you doing? On a Sunday, no less."

"Me? Helping out this kid, Chief."

"This kid?" The chief was a tall, wiry man with a big head of gray hair that appeared to have been blown back by a storm. His skin was pale and spotted with big freckles and the whites of his tired eyes looked smoke stained. "The kid who's a witness to an FDNY truck accident that's going to undergo a full investigation? Where's your head, Doyle?"

"Chief, everyone saw it wasn't us. It was some crazy delivery truck trying to beat the light." Doyle sat up straighter. "Plus, he's got no one else to turn to."

"And this Twitter thing? Using FDNY to raise money? Where's your head? *You* can't just announce you're raising money for someone."

Ryder's stomach sank.

Doyle looked like he'd been hit with a board. "I can't?"

## 12

"There are channels, Doyle. Protocols." The chief narrowed his eyes. "You need a 501(c)(3) and you need *approval.*"

"Yeah, but hey, what about our motto? 'Do the right thing'?" Doyle's fingers began to fidget and he lowered his voice, leaning toward the chief. "This kid's mom needs a heart valve replacement, maybe two, Chief."

The chief grabbed a bulging file from the mess on his desk, opened it, and began yanking out papers stapled together in small stacks. "And we got a captain from Rescue 1 whose daughter needs a kidney, a probie from Engine 18 who needs a bone marrow transplant, and a retired chief with pancreatic cancer they want to send to Sweden for experimental treatment. And the list goes on and on, Doyle. FDNY is like the Nike swoosh, for God's sake. It's a *brand.* Everyone recognizes it. It's famous and it's valuable. And it doesn't belong to *you.*"

Doyle winced and winked and motioned his head toward Ryder.

"I know the kid is sitting right here, Doyle." The chief scowled at the fireman as if Ryder didn't exist. "You brought him here. And is this really where he should be? No. He should be with his *family*."

"That's what this is all about, Chief." Doyle rubbed his mustache, talking faster by the second. "We're working on that. He's got a dad, but they never met. We may know his name. We're gonna look, but that's really it. Well, we got this crotchety neighbor who'll do for a day or so—but otherwise, they're gonna feed him to those ogres at social services."

The chief pressed his lips tight and his face started to color. Each word escaped his mouth like a convict. "My wife works at social services, Doyle."

Ryder could hear the big circular clock ticking on the wall.

Doyle really tugged at his mustache now. "Well, I know that, sir, and she's a fine woman, but she's the exception. You gotta admit. *I* know, Chief. They got hold of me when I was a kid. The old man died and my mom went a little batty and . . ."

"Things have changed immeasurably, Doyle." The chief spoke through his teeth. "Now stop doing other people's job and start doing *yours*."

"But, Chief. We can save this woman's life." Doyle's eyes began to swim. "I told Ryder here I'd do everything I could."

The chief's face softened a bit as he glanced at Ryder, and some of the edge disappeared from his voice. "We can put in the paperwork tomorrow, Doyle, but it'll take some time. There's a lot of people that need saving. You know that."

"She's only got . . ." Doyle looked over at Ryder and swallowed. "The doctors said the next four weeks are pretty important, Chief, less even. Something about insurance, and the whole thing is a mess. Have you seen her?"

Doyle fumbled with his phone, then held up the picture he'd taken of Ryder's mom so the chief could see for himself that this was no ordinary woman.

Ryder eagerly studied the chief's expression.

"Well, it's a long shot, but we'll do the right thing." The chief's eyes broke free from the photo and he looked Ryder's way again, this time for more than a glance. "Of course we will. Got that, son? We'll do our best."

The chief scowled back at Doyle McDonald. "Now, Doyle, you need to get this young man to his neighbor and then you need to get back to work. You've got an inspection first thing in the morning and you know the BITS guys are gonna have to talk with you."

"BITS?" Ryder wrinkled his brow.

"Bureau of Investigation and Trials." Doyle stood up. "Don't worry, buddy. Any time there's an accident, this is what they do."

"It'll all work out." The chief stood up and shook both their hands. "Now, I'm heading back home."

"Sure, Chief."

"Good luck, young man." The chief patted Ryder on the shoulder. "You and your mom."

Doyle and Ryder left without bothering to slide down the pole.

## 13

They returned to Ryder's apartment building.

"Hey, don't give me that look." Doyle shook his head and stopped on the fourth-floor landing where the wallboard had been ripped away, leaving the bare ribs of wood and wires for all the world to see. "I don't want to see that. You gotta think positive, remember? No one wants to see that face."

Ryder shrugged. The scent of mold and wet wood filled his nose. The stairs seemed to creak a little louder than usual and he marveled at the paint chips—big as his hands—peeling away like bark on the sycamore trees in Central Park. Suddenly the stairs seemed tiring and he took a deep breath to fuel his final climb up to the fifth floor.

"It's a lot of money," Doyle said, then quickly held up a finger. "But that doesn't mean we can't get it. When I get back I'll get my inspection stuff finished then start work filling out whatever it is I have to so I can get approvals first thing in the morning."

Doyle went to knock on Mr. Starr's door but stopped, his hand in the air, to look at Ryder. "People talk about miracles happening, but I don't believe that. Miracles are just things that happen right because people didn't stop trying. You gotta try everything, and you gotta believe. Okay?"

Ryder nodded and Doyle let his knuckles fall against the door.

"Who is it!" Mr. Starr's shriek cut through the wood door.

"Doyle McDonald!" Doyle shouted right back. "I've got Ryder."

After a steady electric hum that grew by the second, the lock rattled and the door swung open and there he sat, frozen and twisted, like a smashed car after a very bad accident. "Well? Tell me she's up and about."

Doyle gave Ryder a glance. "No, not really. She's looking good, though. We talked to her, right, Ryder? She's a little out of it, but she's been through a lot."

"What about the father? Did you ask about the father?" Mr. Starr's eyes shifted back and forth between them.

Ryder nodded.

Doyle's mustache sagged. "Well, we're not totally sure because of all the medicine she is on, but she looked at Ryder and was talking about someone named Jimmy and then she said 'Jimmy Trent.' Does *that* ring a bell?"

Mr. Starr's eyes widened.

## 14

"Not with me." Mr. Starr's look of surprise became a glare. "Either you weren't listening, or you already forgot. She told me *nothing*. She left Auburn, New York, when she was pregnant with Ryder here, and never looked back. No names. No mother. No father. No boyfriend, or anyone named Jimmy."

"And Ryder's last name is Strong, so maybe that's it," Doyle said.

"No, that's not it." Mr. Starr seemed to enjoy telling Doyle he was wrong. "She named him Ryder because it means 'warrior on horseback.' The 'Strong' part is just what it sounds like. Strong. She told me that. 'Shoesmith' is the name of some English teacher she had a crush on. Changed her name so they couldn't find her, not that it sounded like they would have ever tried."

Doyle looked at Ryder. "You think 'Trent' is the signature on that baseball?"

"What baseball?" Mr. Starr growled.

Ryder explained that his mom had a signed baseball she kept hidden. "And he called her his gem."

"Well, let's see it, then." Mr. Starr frowned. "Although I can't see how that will help."

"It might help us connect everything." Doyle stroked his mustache. "If it's Trent, then that's gotta be his dad. Okay, I gotta go, but maybe you two could google 'Jimmy Trent' and 'baseball' or something. You want to do that?"

"I have a nurse come into my home every day in the morning and the evening." Mr. Starr spoke calmly and quietly. "I'm fed and clothed and bathed like a broken doll. Do you really think I won't do everything within my mental power to shed the yoke of an abandoned child as quickly as I can?"

Doyle glared. "He's not abandoned. His mother wants him. I'd be glad to have him if I didn't spend half my nights in the firehouse."

Mr. Starr flicked his eyes at Ryder, who was simply too tired to care, and his eyes softened. "No, I suppose that's *not* what I meant. Obviously, I spend too much time alone."

Doyle accepted the shadow of Mr. Starr's apology with a nod, then brightened and snapped his fingers. "Hey, maybe Jimmy Trent still *lives* in Auburn. Maybe there are a family of Trents. Maybe call them and ask for a Jimmy. I don't know. I'm a fireman, not a detective. I gotta go, kid. You'll be okay with Mr. Personality. His bark is worse than his bite, remember?"

"Yeah, I guess," Ryder mumbled.

Doyle got serious. "I'll check back in tomorrow, after my shift, and I'll take you to see your mom. Maybe you should go to school? I'm just saying. . . ."

Ryder shook his head. He couldn't even think about school.

"Okay," Doyle said, "well, be positive."

Then Doyle scooted out the door and down the stairs, leaving behind the fading clunk of his boots and a lot of discomfort.

"Well?" Mr. Starr sounded like he was over being sorry for saying Ryder was unwanted, if he'd been sorry at all.

"Well, what?" Ryder covered up a yawn.

"Get that baseball, and let's get going."

# 15

Ryder did as he was told. It felt strange being in the apartment alone without his mom. The horrible weight of emptiness made it hard to breathe. He hurried into his mom's closet and fumbled with the shoe box, reaching inside without looking, and removed the baseball. He held it up in the thick beam of late-afternoon light streaming through the window. The skin was smooth and yellowing with age; the seams had faded from red to almost pink. The writing was bold and dark, written in black Sharpie, but the signature was a meaningless squiggle.

Ryder turned the ball in his hand. He'd never thought about his father really, never allowed himself to. It seemed traitorous to try and fill in the blanks and give life to a man who'd abandoned his mother . . . and him. But now, now they *needed* to find him—to save her—so Ryder allowed himself to imagine. If he were a baseball player, he'd be athletic, strong, with muscles like tight cables wrapped around long bones. Maybe handsome. Maybe rich?

Ryder sighed, remembering his mother's words, night after night, in the bedroom where he stood. He'd lie in his bed with her snuggled in tight beside him, reading stories about faraway places and fascinating people before she retired to her own bed on the other side of the room. Sometimes he'd wake up with her sleeping there, sitting up with the book open on her lap, and he'd hug her tight and she'd hug him back and stroke his hair. The world belonged to them in those moments and she always said that *they* were rich. Ryder thought she said that to make him feel better. They'd never even been on a vacation. His father, though, he very well could be *rich*.

Ryder looked around the empty room and reconsidered. If he had her back . . . well, he guessed he'd give any amount of money for that, so maybe . . .

He shook his head to break the daze. As he felt around in the box again, his hand swiped at something else at the bottom, something he hadn't told Doyle about, or Mr. Starr. Something he wasn't going to tell anyone about, even though it might hold some clues to finding his father.

# 16

Ryder picked the box up out of the closet and brought it over to his mother's bed. He sat down and the wood frame creaked beneath him. He looked at the dusty box for a minute, trying to decide. The letter made him terribly uncomfortable. No one wanted to see, hear, or read about his parents getting mushy, and this letter was mushy for sure. The first time he'd read it, it gave him the strangest feeling. He hadn't even been sure it was from the man who was his father. He hoped so. Certainly the squiggle of a signature was similar to the one on the baseball.

Ryder took the letter out from the bottom of the box and unfolded it. His fingers rasped against its brittle surface and the paper complained. He took a quick safety glance at the door, even though his mother was in the hospital. He *never* wanted her to know he'd read a letter like this.

It talked about her legs and her hair, her eyes and her lips and kissing. Mushy beyond belief. Sappy like maple syrup, sticky and sweet and messy. Ryder felt his cheeks grow warm, but there was a part of the letter he needed to see again. It had been years since he'd read it and he had to be sure the ending of it wasn't just wishful thinking in his mind. He focused on the last two sentences, written in a script he could only just decipher.

> *You are my beginning and my end, dearest Ruby.*
> *Nothing could make me stop loving you, and so I always*
> *will, now and forever. . . .*
> > *Yours worshipfully,*

And then the signature that might or might *not* be "Jimmy Trent." It could just as likely be "Bartholomew Cubbins," so vague were the squiggly lines. The words proved something to Ryder, though. They told him that whoever wrote it was worth finding, because if what he said was even partly true, this man loved his mother dearly, and likely still loved her, even if he'd lost touch with her over the years. And, Ryder knew instinctively, if the man loved her even a fraction of that, he'd *have* to help save her.

Ryder returned the letter and hurried back to Mr. Starr's with the ball clutched tight in his hand.

"What took you so long?" Mr. Starr asked.

"It was under some things." Ryder raised the ball up in front of the wheelchair.

"Hold it closer." Mr. Starr's lips moved as he read, and the inscription made him snort. "Well, it could say Jimmy Trent, not that that means anything. It could say Kris Kringle."

Mr. Starr looked away from the ball, out the window at the flare of orange where the sun was setting behind the building across the street.

"What do we do now?" Ryder asked after a pause.

"I didn't mean to bore you." Mr. Starr made a sniffing noise, which was strange to hear since his face didn't move when he did it. "Let me get to work. You can stay right here and watch. You look wiped out."

"I am." Ryder stifled a yawn.

"Rest. You'll have to fix your own dinner later."

"I can," Ryder said.

"Tonight, you can stay on my couch if you like, or you really could just stay in your own place if you locked yourself in. I'd be right here. Obviously. It's up to you."

Ryder sat down on the couch, a velvety purple thing pushed against the low wall between the living room and the kitchen. The floors were bare and cold and Ryder suspected that made it easier for a wheelchair. "Is this couch from before?"

The wheelchair buzzed across the floor and stopped right in front of Ryder. "I kissed a lot of girls on that couch."

Ryder wrinkled his nose and couldn't help thinking of the letter in the shoe box. He didn't like talk of such things.

Mr. Starr's mouth curled into a twisted smile. "Oh, I was no looker. A girl like your mother never would have given me a second thought, even in my heyday. But there's a cover for every pot and I sampled my share of covers."

"I'm not really into girls all that much." Ryder scooted to the edge of the couch.

"Good. You will be smitten sooner than is good for you."

"How soon?" Ryder eyed him suspiciously, searching for signs of a joke.

"Soon enough." Mr. Starr buzzed the chair backward and came to rest in front of the naked window. There was a pair of binoculars on the ledge, but he didn't pick them up.

"Smitten?"

"Goo-goo ga-ga. Silly. Distracted. Bananas. Con*sumed*." Mr. Starr moved the chair closer again, to study Ryder's face. "For a pretty face, men do things they never thought they'd do. You know Helen of Troy? The face that launched a *thousand ships*. Tens of thousands of men, off to war, slaughtered because of a woman. That's smitten. Doyle is smitten."

"Doyle?"

Mr. Starr narrowed his eyes. "You think he wants to be the dad of somebody else's twelve-year-old kid? Firemen see car crashes every day. They don't stop everything and play the hero for some four-hundred-pound lady with no teeth and a hyena laugh. It's your mom. You never noticed how she does that to people?"

Ryder did know. He thought of the word "worshipfully" and gave Mr. Starr a startled look. "But why would Jimmy Trent not stay with her? Because of me?"

"She could launch a thousand ships. Maybe ten thousand," Mr. Starr muttered to himself as if he hadn't heard Ryder, then he buzzed his chair over to a desk that had been pushed up against the wall away from the window and the couch. "Oh, dang it. Let me get to work. You should close your eyes."

A computer sat atop the old wooden desk and, using the

jerky motion of his right arm, Mr. Starr managed to press something that brought the screen to life. With a wide sweep, he brought what looked like a microphone on the end of a bendable metal neck so that it stayed within inches of his mouth. He dropped his twisted hand onto a touchpad. Using the combination of a hooked finger on the pad and words he muttered into the microphone, he began to navigate the Web in search for Jimmy Trent.

Ryder leaned over and curled his legs up on the couch. He put his head onto a velvety crimson pillow that matched the cushions on the couch. He was exhausted, and he did close his eyes. As he drifted off, he let his fingers travel up and down the laces of the signed baseball as he filled in more of the blanks of Jimmy Trent, the man he imagined was his father.

# 17

Ryder woke up to the sound of keys rattling in the door. The room was now dark, but for the glow of the computer screen. Ryder bolted up in a bit of a panic. For a brief moment, the intensity of his nap made it seem like the whole thing might have been a dream, but the lights went on and a nurse waddled in.

"Oh! Who are *you*?" she asked, startled.

Ryder blinked. The look on her face told him he wasn't welcome. Naturally shy, he had no words. "Uhhhh."

Mr. Starr whirred around in his chair to face the nurse. "Do you think because I'm entombed in this wreck of flesh and bone that I'm not allowed guests? This is my nephew. His name is Ryder."

Ryder sat silently, absorbing yet another lie about who and what he was with an impassive face.

"Say hello," Mr. Starr barked so abruptly that both the nurse and Ryder said hello at the same time.

"I'm Amy Gillory." The nurse wore a white uniform that barely contained her stout figure, and her arms seemed too short for the barrel of her squat body. Her hair was bluntly cut and dyed a purple-pinkish color. She had big brown eyes set in a doughy white face, and thick, painted lips.

Ryder shook her hand.

"He's shy." Mr. Starr started his wheelchair across the room toward the short hallway that led to an oversized bathroom. "Let's get this over with."

Ryder watched them disappear behind the bathroom door and sat silently, listening to the sounds of water being drawn and washcloths being dipped and wrung out. After a while, Amy Gillory came out in a flurry. Ryder craned his neck around and looked through the opening into the kitchen. On the kitchen counter just inside the front door, the nurse had left a premade dinner tray. She stuck that into the microwave and it hummed while Mr. Starr appeared, whirring along in fresh clothes with his thin strands of hair plastered to his misshapen skull. The intensity of his glare suggested that he didn't like whatever had happened behind the bathroom door, but he said nothing.

When the chair came to a stop in front of the couch, Ryder shifted in his seat. "Do you need me to do something?"

"Can you fix yourself something to eat?" Mr. Starr whispered so the nurse couldn't hear him.

"SpaghettiOs."

"Do you like SpaghettiOs?"

"Yes, would you like some?"

The microwave beeped from the kitchen and the nurse appeared, unfolded a small tray stand with one hand, and expertly set down Mr. Starr's dinner as she plunked herself onto the other end of the couch.

"I have this." Mr. Starr flicked his eyes at what looked to Ryder like a kind of glorified school lunch. "You go have something to eat with the neighbors, and then come back."

Ryder scooted off the couch and addressed the nurse. "Nice to meet you."

"Yup." She didn't even look his way as she spooned a dollop of applesauce into Mr. Starr's mouth, letting her own mouth hang open as she did so, just the way Ryder had seen people feed babies. He wondered why Mr. Starr had to be fed when he could obviously use a computer. Then he realized it was because his elbows wouldn't bend far enough to allow his hands to reach his face.

He got out of there and went back to his empty apartment. He heated up some SpaghettiOs in a pot to have with a glass of milk and two slices of bread thick with soft butter. When he cleaned up and returned to Mr. Starr's, the nurse was gone and he was back at the computer.

"Well, we know you can sleep on the couch without any problems." Mr. Starr worked the touchpad without looking back. "But I want you to get some sheets so your drool isn't all over the place. I drool enough for a classroom of boys, but that's my prerogative. Here . . . look at this."

Mr. Starr gave the computer keyboard a final stroke with a crooked finger and tilted his entire upper body to study the screen from a new angle. Something in his tone suggested great importance.

Ryder snatched his signed baseball up off the couch and clutched it as he crossed the room. "Did you find something?"

## 18

"Well, something, I guess. Auburn, New York, is full of Trents, see them?" Mr. Starr angled his head toward the screen.

Ryder looked at the list on the screen, jittery.

"But no Jameses or Jimmys to be found," Mr. Starr mumbled. "I even made some phone calls."

Ryder's heart sank. He was silent for a minute before he spoke. "You can use that thing to call people?"

"It's the internet, you can use it to perform robotic surgery on someone in Australia, of course you can use it to call people, not that I call people. The people in my life are . . ." Mr. Starr blew air out his nose.

"Why don't you like that lady?" Ryder was thinking of the nurse since she was the only person he assumed Mr. Starr knew.

"Amy *Gillory*? My evening zookeeper? What animal really likes its keeper? I'm not talking about its master. Dogs and cats?

They can love their master, but no animal likes its keeper. In fact, the animal resents its keeper because in the wild, it would fend for itself and that's where it instinctively knows it should be."

Ryder wanted to change the subject. "What did you do? Before . . . you know."

"Before my body turned into a blob of hardened wax? I was a writer. For the *New York Post*."

"A sports reporter?"

Mr. Starr snorted and choked. "Good God, no. I was a crime reporter, which actually requires one to *work*. You can't run down a serial killer's second-grade teacher in a wheelchair. So, they offered me a television column. Can you imagine that? You think people who watch television need someone telling them what they saw? What's good? What's bad? Seriously? It's *television*. I said I'd rather be on half-pay disability than undertake something so meaningless."

"Did you ever write a book or anything?" Ryder asked, still trying to find some solid ground.

"I started one, yes. Then my fingers froze into these delightful claws. Recently, they've come up with some voice programs that almost work, but now that I actually *can* write again, I find I have nothing to say. Obviously there's nothing immediately around me—these four walls and the view out my window— but even in the wide world, the things I read about, I find no inspiration. The world is in a tailspin. Everyone knows that. Everyone writes about it. They don't need me to add to it. More meaningless drivel . . ."

Ryder shifted his attention to the screen and pointed. "Is

that how many James Trents there are?"

"Yes, over three thousand, and that's just on Facebook. None connected to Auburn, New York, though." Mr. Starr clucked his tongue.

"But what about when I was . . . before I was born. Before my mom came to New York City?" Ryder asked.

Mr. Starr made a humming in his nose. "Hmm, yes. I've been checking back over the last thirteen years, landlines and cell phones. Nothing. Look, this Jimmy Trent could have been someone your mom met on a vacation or a school trip or anything. He might not even *be* your father. We're guessing, Ryder. We're grasping."

Ryder's heart suddenly gave him a jolt. "Wait, but what about baseball?"

"I think you need to let go of the pipe dream that your father was or is some kind of sports star. You know the odds of that? If we do find him, he'll probably be working the cash register at a Qwik Fill, and that's if you're lucky."

"But you could check." Ryder didn't want to let it go. "He could have signed it. He might be famous."

"You don't think I checked?" Mr. Starr sounded insulted. "I crossed 'MLB' with that name and every major league team individually. I was an investigative reporter. They don't have those anymore, people just sit in front of their computer screens and gossip, but I know what it is to *find* someone."

"But if you were a sports reporter, you might know that the Toronto Blue Jays have a single-A farm team in Auburn, New York. It's not a major league team. They're called the Double-days." Ryder actually bounced on his feet. "And if I'm a good

65

baseball player because my father was a good player, and she got this ball when she met him, then maybe he was on that team. . . ."

Mr. Starr sucked in his lower lip. "And if he was, he probably wouldn't have had a phone listed in Auburn. Those minor league players are like gypsies. His phone could have been a cell phone from anywhere. He might have lived in a hotel instead of an apartment or a house."

Ryder gave his hands a clap. "And maybe he'd be on the Doubledays roster the year before I was born."

Mr. Starr's finger scratched across the touchpad and he muttered quickly into the microphone. He clicked on a website called Baseball-Reference.com. Another click and up came a headline that read: AUBURN DOUBLEDAYS ROSTER.

Mr. Starr started to scroll down to find the correct year. When he got to the top of the roster and the names starting with *A* through *J,* he paused with his finger above the Down key, looked at Ryder, and took a deep breath.

"You ready?"

## 19

Ryder seemed to float, standing there in the pocket of light in the corner of the dark room next to Mr. Starr. It was like the two of them had been cast adrift in space with only the desk and its computer holding them together. His eyes zoomed in on the roster.

Mr. Starr scrolled down. Ryder saw the last name "Trent," but blinked. It wasn't Jimmy Trent. It was Thomas Trent.

"That's not Jimmy," Ryder said. "Thomas Trent . . . I've heard of him before . . . in baseball."

"I knew a Richard once." Mr. Starr used the touchpad to adjust the cursor over the top of Thomas Trent's name. "Everyone called him Jacob in high school. Then I ran into him years later outside a Broadway play. He was married with kids and calling himself Richard. I had no idea why."

Mr. Starr double-clicked on Thomas Trent's name and a

full player profile filled the screen. "Turns out my friend's *middle* name was Jacob."

Ryder leaned toward the screen. It was just like Mr. Starr said: Thomas James Trent.

"So, is that my father?" Ryder asked.

Mr. Starr clicked on the arrow until he got back to Google. He spoke Thomas Trent's name into the microphone and it appeared in the search box. Then he moved the cursor to "Images" and clicked on that. A gallery of rectangular images popped up on the screen. The ones at the top were all of a baseball player in Atlanta Braves uniforms, either white or gray, a blue hat with a white *A* and a red brim.

Thomas Trent from the Atlanta Braves was one of MLB's top closers, and it all came together in Ryder's mind. He *had* heard that name, even though he wasn't a big Braves fan.

Thomas Trent was rich.

He was practically famous.

And—judging from the resemblance he had to Ryder's own face, dark curly hair, and striking green eyes—he just might be Ryder's dad. The possibility gripped Ryder by the throat and tossed him about until he was dizzy. Thomas Trent was the kind of father he'd secretly wished for all his life. That came out in a flood, the realization that he had ached for a father. Almost any father would have done.

He couldn't help thinking how different his life would have been and how different it might now be, with a father. He realized not having one was a big part of why he'd been so shy and so reluctant to make friends. It was because he felt like something was wrong with him, that he was missing something and not as good as other people. He realized now, amid the raging storm of emotions swirling through him, that if Thomas Trent was his father, Ryder's life would never be the same.

Mr. Starr's hand flopped from the computer touchpad to the arm of his wheelchair and the chair buzzed a quarter turn so that their eyes met.

"You realize, don't you?" Mr. Starr said, as if he'd been able to read Ryder's mind. "This changes everything." Mr. Starr turned back to the computer, muttering. "I know they're having the interleague games early this year; I mean, I know it would be a crazy coincidence, but . . ."

Mr. Starr worked his touchpad and pulled up the Atlanta Braves schedule. "Ha! Talk about fate? They're here."

"Who? Where?"

Mr. Starr spun his chair again so that he faced Ryder. "The Braves. They played the Yankees yesterday and today and they've got an afternoon game tomorrow. First pitch is at 1:05. Your father is in this city somewhere, right now."

## 20

The next morning, the sound of keys in the door again jarred Ryder from his sleep. He bolted up from the couch. The sudden memory of the accident and everything else tilted the room beneath him, but the thought of saving his mother was rocket fuel in his veins, and before he'd fallen asleep on the couch, he and Mr. Starr had devised a plan to do just that.

The door swung open and the morning nurse walked in. This nurse was quite different from Amy Gillory, young and pretty and pleasant, but she didn't seem to know how to react to Ryder.

"Hi, I'm Ashleigh Love." The nurse forced a smile and shook hands with Ryder.

Before Ryder could speak, Mr. Starr's bedroom door burst open and his chair buzzed right out at them.

"And the name fits. Loving and lovely." Mr. Starr wore no

expression, so Ryder didn't know if he was trying to be funny or if he really appreciated Ashleigh's pleasant disposition. "Ashleigh, this is my nephew, Ryder."

Ashleigh nodded at Ryder then turned her attention to Mr. Starr. "Well, are you ready?"

"Don't you love a person who gets right down to business, Ryder?" Mr. Starr's eyes sparkled.

"Sure." Ryder knew nothing else he could say.

Mr. Starr allowed Ashleigh to wheel him into the bathroom without any of the harsh words he'd had for the night nurse. Ashleigh waved back to Ryder, then shut the door and he heard her clucking over Mr. Starr like a mother hen.

Ryder tried not to listen to the sounds of Ashleigh Love cleaning up Mr. Starr to make him ready for the day, but when something happened that caused the nurse to yelp and apologize, Mr. Starr started yelling at her too. Ryder felt his face go hot and he slipped out of the apartment and across the hall to his own place to eat some cereal and put on fresh clothes. When he returned, everything seemed fine. Ashleigh Love fed Mr. Starr his last spoonful of oatmeal before packing up to go.

Ashleigh zipped up her big duffel bag and turned to Ryder. "So, I'll see you tomorrow?"

Mr. Starr jumped in. "You never know with my sister, his mom. Very erratic. Always was. He may come and go a bit. One never knows."

"I didn't know you even had a sister, Mr. Starr," she said.

"There've been many times I haven't known it myself, dear," he said. "I'll see you tomorrow."

When the door closed they looked at each other.

"Nice girl," Mr. Starr said.

"Yes."

"So, you think you can do this?" Mr. Starr's eyes bored right into Ryder's core.

Ryder nodded and knew Mr. Starr was talking about their plan.

"Tell me again," Mr. Starr said.

Ryder ticked on his fingers the steps they'd devised the night before. "I take the subway to Yankee Stadium. I ask a cop where the team bus comes in. I get as close as I can and I shout to Thomas Trent and if I get close, I ask if he remembers Ruby from Auburn. I show him the baseball and hand him the note and tell him I have to speak to him. It's a matter of life and death."

"And that you think you're his son. I want you to say that."

"Really?" Ryder stared at Mr. Starr. Telling Thomas Trent that Ryder was his son was something they'd debated long into the night last night. They'd come up with no answer until, apparently, now.

"Yes. I've been thinking about it." Mr. Starr's eyes seemed to flash. "You have to hit him right between the eyes. Get his attention. That will do it, trust me. If you can, say it so only he can hear, but either way, you've got to say it."

Ryder shrugged. "Okay. I guess I better get going. They get there two hours before the game, right?"

"Sometimes earlier, so don't dawdle. You need to see him today." Mr. Starr banged a crooked hand down on his armrest. "The visitors' bus should pull up to the loading dock near the garage on 164th Street, but don't take that as gospel. I just read it from some crazy fan's online blog about how he gets MLB autographs. The guy might be a total loon for all I know. Ask someone who's there, a cop or a stadium worker or someone. If anyone asks you why, you're just hoping to get an autograph on your ball. No one will bother you that way. You got to wait there where the buses arrive, and just shout to him."

Ryder stared for a moment. "I just hand him the ball and say, 'Mr. Trent, remember Auburn, New York? I'm your son. Ruby's my mom'?"

Mr. Starr blinked. "That's it. That'll get him and then you hand him the note I printed out last night. My email is on it and hopefully he'll reach out."

Ryder patted his pants pocket. Mr. Starr had composed a note meant not to scare Thomas Trent off, but to draw him in.

"Do you think it'll work?" Ryder asked.

"We have to try. He's right here, for God's sake." Mr. Starr pulled open a desk drawer and fished around awkwardly for a minute before producing a thin fold of money. "Use this for whatever you need."

"I can't take your money. . . ."

Mr. Starr shook his head. "I don't need it. *You* might need it. What about the subway? So just take it."

Ryder reached out and took the money. He put a hand on Mr. Starr's shoulder, trying not to recoil at the feel of his frozen frame beneath the white cotton dress shirt that was threadbare and stained around the wrists and collar.

"Oh, go already." Mr. Starr sounded grumpy but his eyes weren't. "And don't forget the ball."

"Thank you, Mr. Starr." Ryder picked the ball up off the

couch and retreated as he struggled into his coat, then let himself out and jogged down the stairs. The morning sun hit him on the street, and even when he closed his eyes, he could feel its energy pushing through the red screen of his lids. The air was crisp and the noises of the city sang softly to him. His heart banged in his chest because he knew—without a doubt—that today would be a day he'd never forget.

# 21

When Ryder came up out of the subway, the wind hit him full force and pushed the tangy smell of the Harlem River up his nose. It was a smell he knew.

He'd been at Yankee Stadium before, having begged his mom every year since he was seven years old to take him to a game for his birthday. They'd arrive by subway and go right into the stadium, sitting in the upper deck along the outfield, the cheap seats. She'd always been a little stiff about it. He had assumed that was because she wasn't a huge baseball fan, but now wondered if it was painful for her because of the connection with his father. He supposed seeing the star players and knowing their salaries would be a tough reminder of just how much she struggled to make ends meet.

He asked an old guy on the sidewalk if he knew where the parking garage was, and the man directed him up the street next to the stadium.

"You gotta go across the street for the parking garage, though." The skin under the old man's chin flapped when he spoke, and he acted like he was chewing on something bitter.

Ryder thanked the man, waited for the light, and crossed the street in a hurry. When he reached the parking garage, he didn't see a way for buses to get in and he didn't see anyone to ask about a loading dock. He hustled up a side street farther than he intended to, then scolded himself for being a chicken. The neighborhood was tougher than his own, and he was nervous. But it shouldn't matter. Wasn't his mom's life on the line? This was a quest, *his* quest. He was like those kids he read about in books about knights and dragons, the quiet kid who kept to himself, but when called upon could commit acts of amazing heroism.

He stood a little straighter, gritted his teeth, and pressed on up the street, hoping to see someone who could tell him if this was the right parking garage, and that's when he noticed two older kids coming directly toward him. One had orange hair cut so close he looked nearly bald and a pale freckled face, flat as a frying pan. The other was shorter and more muscular, with jet-black hair and the small squinty eyes of an attack dog. Ryder's stomach dropped. Something about these two boys was menacing. He looked around for a sign of anyone else—not even a cop, but just another adult.

The only people he saw were two more older kids coming up behind him, one short and fat, like a little Buddha statue, and the other with a nasty growth of fuzz on his face that looked more like mold than hair. Both wore hooded sweatshirts pulled up over their heads so part of each one's face was hidden in shadows. Panic gripped Ryder's throat and his hair stood on end. He crossed the street, hopeful he was just being a scaredy-cat, but the older kids crossed too and he could see the spaces in their crooked, grinning teeth.

Ryder stopped and they did too, four of them now, surrounding him.

"Hey, kid. You ain't from around here." Orange seemed to be their leader.

"No." Ryder could barely speak, and still, a small light of hope shone in the corner of his mind. Maybe they were just teasing.

One of the boys behind him spoke in a slow, guttural voice. "What you got in your pockets? Money for popcorn and peanuts? Maybe a Yankees pennant?"

"Maybe he don't know he's on a toll road?" Orange cocked his head and looked at the attack dog, both of them smirking.

"Oh, yeah." Attack Dog snapped his fingers. "But he won't try to get away with not paying the toll. He look like he a law-abiding citizen. That what you are, boy?"

"I'm just lost." Ryder felt stupid and weak. "I'm looking for where the visiting team buses go."

Orange laughed. "Lost boy."

Ryder wanted desperately to share his secret with them because he felt that if he did, they would let him go, a lost boy looking for the father he never met? These boys looked like they could be missing a father or two among them.

*Snick.*

The gleam of a switchblade startled him. Ryder's knees started to tremble. "What do you want?"

"What you got?" Orange asked.

Attack Dog leered at him and parted open his coat with one hand. Jammed into the waist of his jeans was the handle of his own knife.

Ryder felt tears start to stream down his cheeks as he dug into his pockets and turned them all inside out. The baseball plunked to the sidewalk, then the money and the note Mr. Starr had given him fluttered to the ground.

## 22

"Aww, don't you go cryin'. What are you, a baby?" Orange looked truly disgusted as he snatched up the money, the baseball, and the note. "It's just a toll. Your mommy's gonna get you a pennant anyway. I see it every time."

"My mom is in the hospital." Ryder sniffed. Shame and terror burned his face.

"Your dad, then." Attack Dog let his coat fall back into place and he poked Ryder in the shoulder. "How old you?"

"Twelve. I have no dad."

"Who you with, boy?" asked one of the kids behind him. It was Buddha.

Ryder shrugged. "I'm not. I took the subway. I'm trying to get an autograph from some of the Braves."

"The *Braves*." Behind him, Buddha snorted. "No wonder you're lost. This is New York, boy. What do you want a Braves autograph for?"

"I'm related to one of them." Ryder spoke softly and decided not to say Thomas Trent was his dad. "He's a relief pitcher."

"Sure. Like a cousin?" Attack Dog brightened and put a thumb in his own chest. "My cousin is Rihanna."

"Your cousin's not Rihanna, dip head." Orange glared.

"And his cousin isn't a Brave, that's what I'm sayin'." Attack Dog scowled at Ryder. "Who told you that?"

"A friend . . . of my family."

"What's this?" Orange held up the note Mr. Starr had written and unfolded it.

Ryder couldn't speak. The note would tell these boys everything, and the shame made him sick to his stomach.

"What's this?" Orange growled at Ryder now.

"It's a note to my cousin inviting him to stop by if he wants."

"What, you think you live someplace fancy? Please, boy, you're just like us." Orange threw the note at Ryder and pointed at his shoes. "Look at those kicks you got."

Ryder looked down at faded gray Starters.

Attack Dog laughed. "What'd they cost? Five bucks at the Sav-Mart? You live in some hole an' you're inviting a major league player to your place? That's crazy."

"Look at this ball." Buddha tossed it up and snatched it in the air. "Thing is yellow as snot. Here. We don't need this."

Ryder took the ball and jammed it back into his coat pocket. "Can you guys just let me go?"

Orange shrugged. "We never stopped you in the first place."

The two who had been behind him parted now and stood on either side of him. Ryder picked up the note, turned slowly, and began to walk away. When he looked back he saw them staring, and he took off at a full sprint, running hard, away from the cackle of laughter until he reached River Avenue and bumped square into a cop.

"Whoa. Where you going?" The cop scowled at him harder than the thieves.

"Just . . ." Ryder did a quick calculation, knowing that if he told the cop about the boys it might entangle him like a web he couldn't get out of anytime soon. "I'm trying to get some autographs."

"Ditched school? Got here early, huh?" The cop dusted his jacket.

Ryder nodded. "Someone said the buses come near the parking garage. I'm looking for a Braves player."

"Braves?" The cop screwed up his thick red face. "This isn't the right garage. You gotta head down toward the end of the stadium and they come in off of 164th Street, but I don't know if you'll get any autographs. You can't get that close. There's gates."

"Do they ever come over to the gates?"

The cop scratched up under his cap. "Maybe, but the best place is inside. You want to get in there early and hang out just over their dugout. Sometimes they sign."

Ryder thought of his empty pockets and the stolen money. "I'll just try here. Thanks."

The cop looked up the street and squinted his eyes, pointing. "I think that's probably them right there. Better hurry."

Ryder turned and saw a big luxury bus rumble around the corner and pull into some gates at the back of the stadium.

Ryder took off without a word, running faster than he ever knew he could.

## 23

Sections of thick metal fencing stood linked together, blocking the way into the loading dock area. Two security guards in yellow jackets swung the gates closed. The bus had already come to rest just outside the stadium's back entrance. Players in leather jackets wearing headphones stepped down off the bus and made a beeline for the dark opening that would lead them to their lockers. Ryder was more than a hundred feet away. He looked around, panicked, for a way to get closer. He had an urge to throw himself over the fence—it was only about three and a half feet high—but his mother's training to always obey the rules just wouldn't let him.

He could yell, though, and that's what he did.

"Thomas Trent!" Ryder jumped up and down with the note in one hand and the baseball in the other, aware that a cluster of other autograph hounds had also been drawn toward the fence by the sight of the Atlanta Braves players.

"Trent!" Ryder howled, but either none of the players could hear because of their headphones, or they ignored what to them was just some crazy kid.

"Easy, kid, you'll blow out a lung." A middle-aged man in a dirty leather jacket with a binder notebook full of playing cards took a step away from him.

Then Ryder saw Thomas Trent step down off the bus.

The relief pitcher wasn't wearing headphones.

Ryder's heart hammered against his ribs. The sight of the man who he now knew must be his father choked him so that nothing came out. Thomas Trent turned and headed for the doorway. He had a duffel bag over his shoulder, like the rest. His leather coat was dark brown, smooth and buttery looking, and he wore matching cowboy boots beneath designer jeans. Just as his front foot hit the threshold of the entrance, Ryder erupted.

"TRENT!"

Thomas Trent stopped and turned, looking right at Ryder from across the lot.

## 24

Under the spell of seeing his father, Ryder wasn't even aware that the guards had swung the gates in again, opening them wide. He heard the rumble of the bus and smelled its foul exhaust, but it meant nothing to him compared to the sight of his father and the bright green eyes looking back from beneath an eave of curly black hair that reminded him of his own.

"I'M YOUR S—"

When the bus drove between them, the switch went off. The spell was gone and so was his father.

"Thomas Trent!" Ryder howled and waved the note in the air, but the moment was broken.

One of the security guards, an enormous man with a small, round head, began to wander over toward the fence with his eyes on Ryder.

"Easy, kid." The man with the dirty leather jacket and

binder took another step back. "Get yourself a ticket and go inside. You might get him by the dugout. Sometimes, if you're lucky, the players will sign things there."

"I don't have a ticket!" Ryder's voice sounded hysterical.

"Scalp one. It's the Braves, kid. You can probably get a nosebleed seat for twenty bucks." The man tilted his head.

"They took my money!" Ryder screamed in frustration at the man, startling himself because he couldn't remember ever just screaming at anyone.

"Hey. Kid." The security guard barked at Ryder and kept coming his way. His unblinking eyes were locked on Ryder. It was trouble. Ryder backed up and turned and ran. When he looked back he saw the security guard talking into his radio. Ryder saw some police up ahead and—without thinking—he darted back across River Avenue. A car he didn't see jammed on its brakes as he ran by, squealing sideways, its tires smoking and poisoning the air with burned rubber.

Ryder bolted forward. Another car streaked past, blaring its horn. He made it to the far curb and shot right back down the street he'd been robbed on. Halfway down, he turned and saw no one was following him. There was a steady stream of fans now, but all going the other way, heading toward the stadium. Ryder leaned his back up against the concrete of the parking garage and felt everything crumple. His legs folded and he slumped down until he sat on the concrete with his back against the garage wall.

He hung his head between his knees so no one could see him and began to sob, certain now that he had missed his chance to meet his father, but more important, the chance to save his mother's life. He was no quiet hero. He was a chicken and a flop. He sat for five or ten minutes and cried himself out, aware that people were passing him, and that no one stopped. When he felt a kick against his sneaker, he flinched and looked up through blurry eyes.

It was Orange.

"Hey, you're too old to be cryin' about twenty dollars, boy. Twenty dollars is like three Happy Meals. Ain't no big deal." Orange grinned down at him like they were old friends.

The rest of the gang circled around him.

"Big baby," Buddha muttered, and spit on the sidewalk.

"Twenty bucks?" Ryder screamed up at them, possessed by hopelessness and despair. "I could've gotten a ticket for twenty bucks! You stole my money!"

Ryder hopped to his feet and Attack Dog was on him, smothering his mouth with one hand and the other an iron lock on the back of his neck as the others crowded in, looking around and nervous, even though the stream of people going by all turned their heads the other way.

"No, you don't do that." Orange spoke soft and calm and shook his head. "You wanna get into the stadium? That's what you want?"

Ryder glared at him and nodded and grunted a yes through Attack Dog's hand.

"Well, just say so." Orange smiled at him, talking low, with his freckles mashing together at the seams of his dimpled smile. "We can get you in and you don't need twenty bucks."

Attack Dog removed his hand from Ryder's mouth and loosened the hold on his neck.

"Okay?" Orange spoke quietly.

"You got tickets?" Ryder asked.

Orange snorted and smirked all around. "When you're with us, you don't need a ticket to get into Yankee Stadium. We got a VIP entrance."

The others laughed and exchanged knowing looks. "Yeah."

"VIP?" Ryder wrinkled his forehead.

"Not really VIP. It's more like a *tunnel*." Orange turned and began to walk the other way, against the flow of the crowd. "Come on."

"C'mon, kid." Buddha gave him a light shove. "We'll get you in."

"Yeah." Attack Dog laughed. "We're goin' that way anyhow. You're welcome to join."

Something didn't feel right about this, and every bit of good sense told Ryder to turn and run, but he couldn't. He stood frozen there on the sidewalk as the gang started up the street against the flow of the crowd, but then Orange stopped and winked at him and motioned his chin to follow.

Ryder thought of the major league player inside that stadium—his father—and the pleasant look on his face when their eyes met across the parking lot. Following Orange and his gang was a huge risk, but if Ryder could just have one word with his father, hand him the baseball, and deliver that note, it had to be worth the chance.

Orange turned away, and Ryder yelled, "Wait up!" as he started off after them.

## 25

Just around the corner, a dirty and crumbling apartment building rose up above the storefronts on either side. They circled to
the back of the building and went in through a rotten wood
door. Ryder clutched the iron pipe railing as they descended
into the dark. Where are we going? he thought to himself as
the steps wavered beneath him. He followed the gang down
into a basement that stank like nothing Ryder had ever smelled
before. Toilet water gone bad mixed with puke and dog poop
was all he could think of as he forced air from his throat up into
his nose to keep the smell from getting in. Still, he could taste
it as he breathed through his mouth. He had to breathe. The
older boys in front of him talked and laughed like it was nothing, and he remembered learning in science class that if you
smelled something long enough, you stopped smelling it at all.

His feet hit the cool concrete floor. Up ahead, one of them
flicked on a flashlight. Ryder heard small splashing sounds.

Above, cobwebs thick as spaghetti hung limp from stained and moldy wooden beams. White plastic pipes and rusted iron ones crisscrossed each other, some hung by coat hangers and others by plastic collars. Ryder tried to step carefully through the shallow pond of bad water, the maze of hulking boilers and discarded appliances, and up through a broken brick wall into a man-sized black hole. The tunnel turned to dirt packed so tight it looked gray in the flicker of yellow light up ahead.

It was impossible to believe, but the smell got worse, thick and hot so that Ryder had to concentrate hard to keep the cereal he'd had for breakfast in his stomach. They stepped out of the tunnel onto a concrete walkway and turned left. Below the walkway, a river of filth slogged silently along the bottom of a bigger tunnel. With every step, Ryder's imagination haunted him with the idea that he was headed to his own grave. He heard the squeak of a rat that scurried over the top of his shoe before skittering along crumbling concrete. He looked at the empty blackness behind him, thinking that by now they must be under the stadium, or even past it, approaching the Harlem River.

The walkway suddenly ended at a metal door and the five of them crowded up to it while Attack Dog held the light and Orange stuck something into the rusted keyhole, then cranked the handle. They slipped through and their voices became hushed. Orange held the door, looked back at Ryder, and mashed a finger to his lips. Ryder nodded that he understood, and followed Orange through the door.

They came to a metal ladder and up they went with only the sound of their feet dinging the rungs as they passed through a concrete tube and stepped up onto the floor of a room crowded by a maze of piping thick as tree trunks. A steady hum filled the space and Ryder swallowed the fresh air that poured in from somewhere above. Orange worked on the lock of another metal door that led into a vault where a pump the size of two city buses churned and growled.

Halfway across a narrow metal bridge, Orange stopped and turned back, holding out a sports headband for Ryder.

"What?" Ryder whispered.

"Put this over your eyes. This is a secret. Don't worry, I'll lead you."

"What do you mean?" Ryder asked, scared to death.

"Don't worry. We just can't have anyone knowing how we do this. No one's gonna hurt you. Come on."

Ryder swallowed and nodded, knowing he had no choice. He was too far in. He pulled the band over his eyes and followed the rest of the way. Someone spun him around and led him through a few bends and doorways before Orange pulled the band off.

"See? Easy."

They piled into the bottom of a stairwell and when Orange closed a massive door, the pumps became nothing but a hum. The five of them started up the metal stairs. On the floor above, huge fire doors tattooed with red warning signs stood ready to burst open in an emergency. They went up another flight, then Orange jimmied that door and motioned for Ryder to come forward.

With a hand on the back of Ryder's neck, Orange leaned close enough for his lips to tickle Ryder's ear. "See how this tunnel goes?"

Ryder nodded because he could see through the crack that

the big, wide hallway went about twenty feet before turning a sharp right.

"So," Orange whispered, "you go down that way and make the right. Then go down two more doors on your left, and take that second door, and when you get through there you'll be in the concession area and no one will even see you in the crowd."

"Where are you going?" Ryder's insides trembled like Jell-O.

Orange chuckled softly. "We got some business. You just get on and go give your cousin a kiss for me."

"What if someone stops me?" Ryder asked.

"No one's gonna stop you," Orange said. "Now get going before I change my mind about being so nice."

Orange tightened his grip on Ryder's neck, widened the crack, and shoved him out into the cinder-block tunnel. Ryder looked back but the door had already been closed. He didn't trust the people who'd just robbed him. He knew something was wrong, but it looked like the tunnel truly was inside the stadium, and maybe he really could get into the crowd where he'd be safe. He started cautiously down the hallway, got to the corner, and peeked around it, seeing that there were two doors on the left. He grew hopeful that the second door really would take him where Orange said it would.

He stepped carefully around the corner and started walking softly down the hall. He was halfway between the two doors on the left when a door farther down on the right swung open and two men dressed in baseball uniforms burst into the hallway.

Ryder froze.

# 26

Instinctively, Ryder flattened himself into the recess of the doorway on his right.

Even as he did, he realized the players' backs were to him. They talked and laughed, and then their voices faded away. He peeked around the edge of the doorframe, eyeing the exit he needed to escape through, but the players' door burst open again. Without thinking, he yanked on the handle poking into his back and slipped inside the door.

He pulled the door shut and stood in total blackness. The voices grew closer this time and two people passed him by. His heart beat wildly. He listened for nearly a minute, but just as he reached for the handle, he heard more people in the hallway. When their voices faded, he told himself it was time to make his break.

He turned the handle and slowly eased his head through the crack.

The door down on the right burst open again, banging the cinder block wall. Ryder ducked back inside. The sound of his breathing kept him company as he tried to imagine why players kept coming out every other minute from the door up the hall. He sat listening for a while before he realized that the door must open into the players' clubhouse.

With his hands out in front of him feeling blindly, he moved through the dark space. He bumped his way through a maze of boxes stacked from the floor to as high as he could reach and realized he'd entered a storage room. He felt his way forward and to the left, in the direction of the room the players had emerged from. When he reached a wall, he didn't have to go far before he felt the cold metal of another door. He put his ear to it and could clearly hear the sound of men talking and joking. It had to be the locker room. Every so often, there would be the bang of a door. He suspected it had to be the one that led out into the hall.

Ryder knew for certain the players' lockers must be just beyond this door. He felt the handle and turned it carefully. It was unlocked.

His legs trembled and sweat broke out on his upper lip as he listened to the sound of the locker room emptying out. He had to pee now, more than he'd ever had to before in his life. He grabbed his own face and squeezed it, unable to believe he was hiding in a storage closet outside a players' clubhouse in Yankee Stadium. It seemed impossible.

When the talking finally stopped on the other side and the last voices faded through the banging door, Ryder turned the knob and peered into the clubhouse. In front of him were all the lockers, and he knew by the colors of the travel bags lying around on the bottoms of the big open lockers that this was the

Braves' visiting locker room. Off to his right were the showers, toilets, and sinks. Ryder thought for a moment about dashing in, finding Thomas Trent's locker, dropping the note, and bolting out of here.

The excitement of that possibility, though, made his urge to use the bathroom so great he thought he'd explode before he took ten steps, so instead he dashed into a stall and took care of business. He was zipping up his pants when he heard someone cough behind him, then footsteps clacking along the bathroom floor tiles.

Ryder froze, then realized, as the footsteps kept getting nearer, that his feet would be seen beneath the stall door. He climbed up onto the toilet, stood on the rim of the bowl, and tried not to even breathe. The steps stopped two doors down and whoever it was rattled the knob and swung open the door.

"Ahhh! Whew! Oh, that *stinks*!" The man, talking to himself, slammed the stall door shut.

Now, his footsteps moved up the line of doors, past the one next to Ryder's and stopping right outside his door. He could see the tips of the man's cleats and guessed that one of the players must have returned to use the bathroom. Ryder stared at the door and bit into his lip to keep from crying out. His legs began to shake again, this time so violently that he realized he might slip right off the rim of the bowl.

The knob rattled and turned. Ryder wondered if he could reach across the open space and flick the lock. He braced his hand against the wall and started to lean. It was his only chance.

But even as he reached for the latch with his other hand, a crack of light appeared in the door and it began to sneak open.

# 27

A foot of open space gaped in front of Ryder. He could see the edge of the player's body and the left arm of his uniform, but the door stopped before it reached his face.

"No. Too close. Aw, that smell is terrible." The door swung shut again and the player went into the next stall over.

Ryder sniffed the air and realized now that there was a bad smell coming from a few stalls down.

A belt buckle clinked against the floor in the stall next to Ryder as the player's pants dropped down around his feet. The feet turned around and the player sat down. Ryder stood like a statue, so scared he couldn't even feel his legs.

Thankfully, the player was in a hurry, so it wasn't long before the toilet flushed, the belt jingled up, the door creaked open, and footsteps clacked across the tile floor and faded around the corner. When the locker room door banged in the next room, Ryder hopped down, let himself out, and crept into the locker room again. The second locker he looked at had the name THOMAS TRENT written on the nameplate above. Ryder's hands shook like October leaves in a windstorm as he pulled the note from his pocket, smoothed it, and set it down onto the stool in front of his father's locker alongside a Braves batting glove.

He reached for the glove because something told him to take it, and that, in a way, it belonged to him. The baseball was really his mother's, and didn't he deserve something for himself? His mother's voice sounded an alarm in his brain, reminding him that stealing was stealing, no matter what. He let his hand drop, set the note on the stool, and turned to go. He took one step before he turned and snatched up the Braves glove again, cramming it into his pocket. He went out the way he came in, through the storage closet. At the door leading into the main hallway, he listened, heard nothing, and eased it open.

The hallway was empty.

Relieved and emboldened, he slipped out of the storage closet and hurried down the hall toward the door on the left that would set him free into the crowd. He thought now that he'd still try and talk to Thomas Trent from above the dugout, but he was already glowing with the knowledge that the note had been delivered. Mr. Starr was a real writer, a professional. His note would certainly convince Thomas Trent to connect with Ryder and then to help his mom. After all, the letter Thomas Trent had written said nothing could make him stop loving her. It said he *worshipped* her, and Ryder told himself that feelings like that didn't just end.

Bubbling with joy and his face decorated with a giant smile, he opened the door and burst into a small welcome party of grim-faced stadium security guards.

# 28

The guards all wore black uniforms and gold badges, with guns and batons fixed to their shiny black belts. "Hey, you! What are you doing?" The one nearest to Ryder's right grabbed him by the collar and held him up enough so that his toes barely danced on the floor. She seemed stouter and stronger than the men she worked with and she forced him around and mashed his face into the wall. Another guard had him spread his hands against the painted cinder blocks before patting him down.

"He's clean."

The guard who had him by the collar spun him back around and now Ryder realized they had Attack Dog too, only his hands were zip-tied behind his back.

"What's that?" The woman guard held Ryder with one hand and pointed at her partner with the other.

"That's my mom's baseball," Ryder said.

"Not that old yellow thing," the woman said.

"Looks like a Braves batting glove." The guard held the glove he'd taken from Ryder's pocket up in the air and turned it over. "Hey, it's got Thomas Trent's name on it. The pitcher."

The woman guard shook Ryder. "You were in the locker room?"

Panic pumped a gusher of words from Ryder's mouth and he started his rambling explanation. "I had to give him a note. I left it at his locker. My mom's real sick. I gotta talk to him. I saw him but a bus came so I had to get in and these guys said they had a tunnel and . . ."

Orange—who also stood with his hands zip-tied—and Attack Dog glowered hatefully at Ryder. He swallowed and stopped talking, then looked nervously back and forth between the guards. One of them ducked out through the doorway Ryder had come through and returned half a minute later with Ryder's note.

"See?" Ryder brightened with the thought they might believe him, know he wasn't really a thief, put the note back, and let him go.

The looks on their faces sank that ship in an instant.

A city cop suddenly appeared in their midst. "What's going on?"

The woman spoke for them all. "We've been after this gang for a while. They get in somehow and send a young one up the main hall. We see him on the cameras and grab him and then they raid the supply room. We didn't even know how the stuff was going missing, but we figured it out and this time we were waiting. They got away with a couple thousand dollars' worth of stuff already."

"Well, it's not good," the cop said, "but I don't want to use up a squad car on some petty thieving. You all can take them in."

"Oh yeah?" The woman guard tilted her head and wore a thin smile. "What about this?"

She held up the knife Ryder had seen in Attack Dog's pants. Attack Dog glared at the woman, then the cop.

The cop let out a low whistle.

"Threatened to use it." Another guard spoke from behind them.

"First-degree robbery," the cop said.

The woman reached into her back pocket. "The other one had a knife too."

The cop looked at Ryder. "What about him? He the decoy?"

Attack Dog suddenly erupted. "He's the one who planned it all. Said he could get us some free stuff."

Ryder's mouth fell open. "Wait, what?!"

"Went right into the locker room and stole a Braves batting glove. Got guts." The woman nodded.

"Got no brains," the cop said. "I'll meet you out at the loading dock, take them to the station in my car, and get them booked."

"Come on, you." The woman who had a hold of Ryder shoved him away from the door he'd come through and down another hallway.

Two other guards had Attack Dog and Orange by their collars, only they stumbled more because of their hands being cuffed behind their backs.

"Really, I'm not with these guys." Ryder tried to talk so the woman guard could hear him but the others couldn't. His mind kept telling him that no matter how she looked, a woman would still have some sympathy for a lost boy trying to save his own mom.

"Quiet, you." The guard led him down the hallway, toward the light from the stadium. Just before they reached an entrance that led out to the field, they took a sharp right and filed down through a curving concrete tunnel. A man in a Yankees uniform appeared from around a corner and bumped into the woman guard and Ryder. The woman stumbled and Ryder went right down, hard on his butt.

"Oh my gosh. I am so sorry." The man helped Ryder to his feet even as Ryder began crying. "Hey, buddy. You okay?"

Ryder saw that—despite the uniform—the man was too old to be a player. The close-cut hair sneaking out from beneath his cap was already gray, but the tan face and big dark eyes were familiar.

"It's our fault, Mr. Girardi." The woman guard snatched Ryder's arm. "We got some thieves here. NYPD is meeting us at the loading docks."

"Thieves?" Joe Girardi, the Yankees manager, looked Ryder up and down. "He's what, thirteen? Fourteen?"

"Twelve," Ryder croaked.

"Well, come on." Joe Girardi frowned. "What did he take?"

"These others have been stealing from the supply room. Uniforms. Bats. Gloves." The woman gestured at Orange and Attack Dog. "The kid was with them. Took a batting glove."

Joe Girardi gave the older boys a blank look, then nodded. "Okay. Well . . . can you just let the kid go, though? I mean, an old batting glove? He doesn't look dangerous. He doesn't even look like he belongs with these characters."

Joe Girardi gave each of the guards the flat empty stare of someone who was used to being obeyed.

Ryder held his breath and wondered if this was the miracle he needed.

## 29

"Of course, Mr. Girardi." The guard's concrete face softened. She smiled and nodded her head, but kept a tight grip on Ryder. "I'll have to see him out, though. Hey, good luck today."

Joe Girardi looked at Ryder again and gave him half a smile along with a wink before he disappeared, walking down, deeper into the tunnel until his pin-striped uniform got swallowed by the gloom.

"Let's go." The woman guard's voice became harsh again, and she didn't stop being rough with Ryder, even when they stood on the loading dock together with her fist wrapped up tight in his coat collar.

He thought about telling her that he'd let Mr. Girardi know if she didn't cut it out and get her hands off of him, but decided to keep quiet.

"Can I have my ball back?" Ryder was emboldened by the

power of the Yankees manager.

The guard who had the ball shrugged and handed it to him. He stuffed it deep in his jacket pocket, trying not to grin at the woman who still held him.

The cop car pulled up and the other guards along with the cop loaded Orange carefully into the backseat along with Attack Dog. The cop stood and turned to the woman guard.

"What about him?"

"Mr. Girardi said to let me go." Ryder couldn't help blurting it out because he didn't like the look he saw on the woman's face.

"Get in there." The woman shoved Ryder toward the car door as if the whole thing with the manager had never happened. "Joe Girardi. Get a load of this kid. I bet Santa Claus put in a good word, too, huh?"

The other security guards snickered along with her, making it seem like he was simply a liar, and the cop put him in, telling him he better keep his hands to himself or he'd be wearing cuffs like the other two. Ryder couldn't even speak. It was so wrong.

"But . . . but . . ." He could only sputter and stutter as the cop got in behind the wheel and began to pull away. The laughter of the stadium security guards roared through the glass of the police car's window.

# 30

The police unloaded them outside a faceless brick government building. Ryder was separated from the others and taken down an empty hall to a small windowless room with a bench screwed into the floor.

"You need the bathroom?" the policeman said.

Ryder shook his head no.

"Okay. Wait here," the police officer said, closing the door.

Ryder sat in silence. All he could think about was his mom. The moment she fell into the street wouldn't stop repeating itself in his head. Tears spilled down his cheeks. He tried to be brave, but ragged sobs escaped him when the torment was too great. Finally, he was too tired to cry, but the image of her in that moment—annoyed with his resistance—kept at him.

It was a long, agonizing time before a guard came and took him out of his holding cell. Orange and Attack Dog stood there in the hallway outside, waiting, and scowling at a guard of their own. They were all marched down a series of hallways, up an elevator, through a back room, and into the courtroom before the judge. Lights from above glimmered off the judge's bald head. Big angry eyes stared out at the boys over the tops of his black-rimmed reading glasses. Rolls of fat cascaded below his ears, piling up on his shoulders like fallen cake dough so that he had no neck at all, and the rolls seemed to flow right into the billows of his black robe.

The judge's hands poking out from the drooping sleeves seemed small for the rest of his bulk, the hands of a puppeteer maybe, standing in the tent of clothes and making motions with stubby fingers that bore no rings. The fingers scooped up some papers and the judge studied them through his glasses before returning his gaze to the boys.

"All right. The Bridge is full, so you two . . ." The judge looked back at the papers. "You're sixteen, so you'll go to Rikers Island. And you."

The judge whipped off his glasses and the dark furry caterpillar eyebrows sloped and met above his nose in a V. "I am sick of seeing twelve-year-olds in here committing crimes with *deadly weapons.* Do you know that a child is injured or killed by a gun in this country every *thirty seconds*! Well? Did you know?"

Ryder couldn't speak, could barely shake his head. He couldn't believe any of this was happening.

The judge pounded his bench with a mini fist. "Well, *I* know, and I'm done with it. This is armed robbery, gentlemen, and I don't care that one of you is twelve and I don't care that you've got some sob story about mama in the hospital."

The judge stared hard, and Ryder could barely breathe. The judge waved the glasses back on his face and looked down at the papers again. He began sifting through some others. "No room here. No room there. I tell you where I got room. I got room at Tryon Residential. How about that, son? Maybe you go see some hard-timers and you get it figured out before you come back here for your trial."

"Your Honor, I don't think a boy twelve years old ought to be in Tryon, and there weren't any guns. I grant you, two of the suspects had *knives*, but my client did not." The woman who'd spoken stood at a table behind Ryder. She had lots of wavy hair and a wide, smooth forehead. She wore a gray business suit with a white blouse and had glasses of her own. Her scowl was just as strong as the judge's. "This boy would be released to his parents under normal circumstances."

The judge's mouth moved as though he were chewing a bit of paper stuck in his teeth. Then he spoke. "You call three kids with a knife normal, Ms. Angie Diles? Nothing normal about that. Tryon was good enough for Mike Tyson, wasn't it? Where's he now? A movie star, so the place has its merits."

Angie Diles shook her head and grunted with disgust.

"Well, did you send anyone over to the address he gave?" The judge seemed to be giving in a bit.

She shook her head. "No one there. The school said he skipped today and they confirmed the mother's name. She *is* in the hospital in critical condition."

Ryder wondered about Mr. Starr and whether they tried talking to him or he scared them off or maybe just gave up on Ryder as a loser.

"And you'd have me do what with this boy, Ms. Diles?" the judge asked.

"A foster home."

"A foster home." The judge blew out his cheeks. "Do you know Deshawn Harper? Does that name ring a bell with you?"

Angie Diles frowned and her lips disappeared into the flat line of her mouth, but she didn't give away if she'd heard the name or not.

The judge nodded. "Boys with knives have already crossed a line. I tried to put Deshawn in a foster home and I won't even tell you what he did to another child they had in that household. We all have our jobs to do, and I don't mind you doing yours, but don't push me on this one, Angie."

The two of them stared each other down. The courtroom went totally silent. Ryder clenched his teeth, sensing something big in the balance.

Suddenly, Ryder heard the courtroom doors burst open behind them, and someone shouted at the judge.

"Wait!"

# 31

Ryder turned and didn't think he'd ever been happier to see someone. Doyle McDonald stood tall and straight, his mustache quivering. Behind him was Derek Raymer.

"I'm sorry, Your Honor. My name is Doyle McDonald. I'm with FDNY, but also a close friend of this boy's family." Doyle spoke as he walked up the center aisle of the courtroom, stopping once he got alongside the table where Angie Diles stood. "There is a neighbor who regularly watches Ryder and lives next door. He doesn't have a phone, so he's hard to get a hold of."

Angie Diles ruffled her papers. "Would that be a Mr. Starr?"

"Yes! Exactly!" Doyle clapped his hands and nodded vigorously. "So, if Your Honor will agree, I can take Ryder. I'm sorry I didn't get here sooner."

"Well . . ." The judge's face softened and so did his voice. "I lost a brother on Nine-Eleven. Ladder Three."

The courtroom went totally silent.

Doyle bowed his head for a moment. "Your Honor. I can vouch for Ryder. I heard what happened and I promise you, when this all gets worked out, the court will see that he's a good kid who was simply in the wrong place at the wrong time."

The judge nodded. "Ms. Diles? This works for you?"

"Of course, Your Honor."

The judge thought for a minute. "Well, Ms. Diles is an officer of the court. Would you agree to check in with her on a daily basis and keep her updated as to the boy's whereabouts?"

"Yes, Your Honor," Doyle said.

The judge thumped his gavel. "Then I remand Ryder Strong to the custody of Mr. McDonald, to be brought to Mr. Starr until Ms. Diles can work out something permanent if that becomes necessary."

"Thank you, Your Honor." Doyle took Ryder by the arm and gently led him toward the door.

They met up with Derek Raymer and left the courtroom, closing the doors behind them. As they marched down the steps, Ryder saw a pickup truck at the curb with its hazard lights flashing. He followed the two firemen and climbed into the front seat between them. Derek got behind the wheel and when the doors were closed, he switched off the hazards and put the truck in gear.

Derek Raymer started, "I don't know about this. You're not a close family friend." Derek shook his head as he made a turn. "You just met these people. At an accident."

Doyle waved a hand impatiently. "Derek, there's right and

there's right. Sometimes the rules aren't right, and when that happens, you gotta just trust your gut and do what's *really* right."

Ryder nodded because he sure understood that, and it was a relief to hear something so sane spoken by an adult.

"Okay, but I just hope your gut doesn't get us fired." Derek smiled apologetically. "I'm just saying."

"Don't you get what *I'm* saying?" Doyle looked across at his friend.

"Sure I do, Doyle, but rules are rules. Look at the mess you got into trying to raise money for the kid's mom."

Doyle shot his partner a hard look.

"What do you mean? What happened with the money?" Hope hung from Ryder's words.

# 32

Doyle huffed. "Nothing. It'll be fine, I'm . . . it's a setback, that's all."

"You're having trouble with raising the money?" Ryder tilted his head, his stomach twisting.

"I'm just still working on it is all." Doyle kept his eyes on the street.

"Working on it?" Derek rolled his eyes.

"That's right, I am, Derek. Enough." Doyle glared at his partner.

"I just happen to like having a job, Doyle," Derek muttered.

"Stop being Negative Nancy," Doyle said. "One thing at a time. We gotta get my guy home."

Derek shook his head. "We were coming to *visit* him? Remember?"

Derek looked at Ryder and smiled sadly. He turned away,

sighed, and shook his head, and then they drove in silence.

As they crossed over the Harlem River, Ryder asked, "Doyle, can you take me to see my mom?"

Ryder saw Derek give Doyle a sharp look, but Doyle laughed another time. "Sure, I can. Let's go there right now."

Derek huffed. "Would you mind dropping me off at the firehouse?"

"Can I use your truck?"

"Of course you can, but don't double-park it."

When they reached the firehouse Derek mussed Ryder's hair before hopping down and wishing them luck. Doyle circled around and got in behind the wheel.

"He's nice." Ryder watched Derek wave in the side mirror.

"The best." Doyle looked around and did a U-turn.

"He's not too happy about all this, though," Ryder said.

"Derek's just cautious. That's why he and I are a good team."

"I hope you won't get into trouble." Ryder meant that.

"Trouble's my middle name." Doyle sped up to make a light. "So, you gonna tell me what the heck you were doing at Yankee Stadium with a bunch of thugs?"

Ryder's stomach clenched. He'd almost forgotten about how he and Mr. Starr had kept all that from Doyle.

He hung his head. "Mr. Starr found my dad."

"Oh, right." Doyle laughed, but not in a funny way. "Kid, don't even dream about your dad being a Yankee. That Starr is pulling your leg. He's a mean cuss if he told you that. It's a pipe dream and he shouldn't have led you on. There's no Jimmy Trent on the Yankees."

"He's not a Yankee." Ryder shook his head.

113

"Oh." Doyle looked over. "Good. What, then? Ticket-taker?"

"He's a Brave. An Atlanta Brave. They played the Yankees in an interleague game."

"Ryder, the Braves' pitcher is *Thomas Trent*, not Jimmy Trent. I'm sure that cranky old fart just googled the name 'Trent' and 'MLB' and came up with him. And then he sent you to that *stadium*?" Doyle ground his teeth. "I don't care if he is in a wheelchair. I'm gonna give that Starr a shake-up."

Ryder shook his head and pulled the baseball from his coat pocket. "No, he *is* my dad, Doyle. He met my mom in Auburn, where she was from. He played for the Doubledays, it's a minor league team. That's where he signed this ball for her. Everyone called him Jimmy, but his name is Thomas James Trent. I *saw* him at the stadium. I looked right at him across the parking lot . . . and he smiled."

Doyle bit his lip. "Well . . . it's possible, but you can't be *certain*."

Ryder frowned and turned away.

"Hey, don't shut me out like that. I'm not the enemy. I just don't want you to be crushed if this doesn't work out. We're making a lot of assumptions here."

Doyle parked the truck in a garage and they crossed the street to the hospital.

Every step closer they got to his mom's room seemed to add a weight to Ryder's heart. When Doyle asked at the desk if they could go into her room, the nurse gave him a serious look and said she'd have to see.

When she disappeared, Doyle nodded his head toward

114

the hallway, silently motioning for Ryder to follow. "You wait around for these medical people and they give you a bunch of rules. Come on. You can see your mom."

The room had a big glass window looking out into the hall, but the glare from the lights didn't allow them to see her well, only the shape of a person in a raised bed. When Doyle put his hand on the door and swung it open, Ryder's knees nearly buckled.

He had no idea what they'd find.

## 33

The sight of the tubes that snaked up into his mother's nose brought tears to Ryder's eyes. He just knew that couldn't be good. The machines beside her bed played their beeping and whirring tunes, blinking red and green in time to the noise. The crease in the sheet folded down below her shoulders rested perfectly, suggesting no movement at all. Her tan skin had a hint of green.

He choked. "Mom?"

She didn't move.

He crept close as Doyle circled the bed, frowning. He touched her cheek with the back of his fingers. The tubes hissed like deadly snakes.

"Mom?" He looked at Doyle, his face rumpling.

Doyle pointed at a small black screen lit by green squiggles of light that followed the path of a bright dot, skittering like a water bug up and down and across the screen. "That's her heartbeat."

"Is it good?" Ryder's voice shook.

"It's there." Doyle's mouth was a flat line.

Ryder brushed some hair from her forehead. "Mom?"

Her eyes fluttered, then opened. She looked at him, her eyes dialing into focus. Then she smiled, and her lips moved. "Ryder."

Sunshine poured into Ryder's heart. "Mom, we're going to get you better. You need an operation, but Doyle's helping me and Mr. Starr. Doyle's raising money. The fire department's helping and . . . and . . . I think I found him, Mom."

"Found who, honey?" He could barely hear her groggy whisper, and didn't know if the wince of pain was from speaking or the subject he was speaking of.

Ryder glanced at Doyle, who also winced.

Ryder held his breath, then exhaled the name. "Jimmy Trent."

His mom closed her eyes, and her face went slack. Ryder's attention jumped to the machines. Everything stayed the same, a steady beep and the steady wave of green lines going up and down.

"Mom?" He put his hand on her forehead.

The door opened behind them. A nurse came in and went right to the machines.

"Is she all right?" Doyle rounded the bed and put a hand on Ryder's neck.

"Well, she's on a lot of morphine, so she fades in and out," the nurse said, glancing over her shoulder. "You'll have to talk to the doctor about everything else."

The doctor had already entered without a sound. "Ah, are you the family?"

"We are." Doyle nodded. "I mean, he is. Her son. I'm a close friend."

The doctor frowned and glanced at Ryder. "So, we need to talk."

## 34

They followed the doctor down the hallway, past other ICU patients tilted up in front of their own windows. They entered a lounge where a small family huddled around a table in the corner. An older lady sniffled and choked back tears as the others patted her back and offered soft words.

"Coffee?" The doctor raised his eyebrows at Doyle and slipped a dollar bill into a vending machine that rattled out a cup then spurted a stream of coffee.

Doyle held up a hand to say no. The doctor got his coffee and sat down across from them at a small table. He sighed before he looked at them. "I presume you've got other family on their way?"

Doyle shook his head. "Ryder here is pretty much it. He's staying with a neighbor."

The doctor had a young face, but his eyebrows were thick,

and dark like the shadow on his jaw, and he knit them together. "I'll have our admin make a call to social serv—"

Doyle cut him off with a hand. "I got that covered. I'm with the FDNY. We brought her in and I know the drill. He's okay for now. We're hoping that you guys can get her well and out of here soon. Meantime, the neighbor is fine."

"Well, that's the problem." The doctor rubbed the scruff of his unshaven face so that it rasped loudly. His eyes skipped over Ryder to Doyle. "I don't know how much the ER doctor told you."

"That she needs a valve replacement. Actually, two valves." Doyle spoke in a low voice. "And insurance won't cover it? Is that true? I mean, she looks tired, but good."

"Yes." The doctor nodded. "She does look good for someone who got hit by a truck, on the outside. The problem is on the inside. When she got hit, it severely bruised her heart and damaged the valves. She won't get better."

"What?" Ryder whispered. The horror of it made Ryder's ears ring. He gripped the edges of his chair to stay upright.

"I just don't understand this insurance thing." Doyle softly pounded his fist on the table.

The doctor shook his head. "Well, here's the problem. Ruby was actually in here about ten years ago."

"She was?" Ryder had no idea.

The doctor nodded. "Yes, she's in our system. Had her tonsils out, actually, and while she was here she filled out a DNR."

"DNR?" Ryder looked at Doyle, whose face had suddenly fallen.

"Do not resuscitate." Doyle spoke softly.

"Right now, for Ruby to have a valve replacement would technically be elective surgery. She won't *need* the valves until her heart fails. . . ."

"But," Doyle said, staring intently at the doctor, "when her heart fails, she's got a DNR that won't let you bring her back. But she can change that, right?"

"If she were coherent, yes," the doctor said. "It's all about timing. If we take her off the morphine, the pain alone would stress her heart tremendously. She might not come out of it. She's like a . . ."

"A time bomb." Doyle immediately looked sorry he'd said the words.

The doctor nodded. "I know it's disturbing, but that's right. I'm sorry."

"So, some people get to *buy* their life if they've got two hundred thousand dollars lying around, but the rest of us die?" Doyle growled.

The doctor shook his head. "No. That's not true, but in this instance, with these facts and the DNR, there's no one who will pay for the transplant until her heart actually stops.

"Honestly? Having two valve replacements isn't a walk in the park. So, even if she hadn't signed the DNR, she'd still be in a bad spot."

"But with the DNR, she's . . . it's . . . ," Doyle said. "But, if we had the money . . ."

"Hey, there was a woman last year who made it like this for six months." The doctor was trying too hard. "And miracles happen every day, so . . ."

"But, what's real?" Doyle asked. "How long can she go

without the new valves? A month?"

The doctor sucked in his lower lip and shook his head as he lowered his voice. "No, not with the way this is going. Honestly, I'd say two weeks. Maybe three."

## 35

They left in a daze.

Ryder rested his head against the truck window, listening to Doyle argue frantically on the phone about using the FDNY name to raise money. He was talking with his union rep, urging him to fight the department on his behalf. It sounded like he was getting nowhere.

"Okay. Okay, but you'll try, right? You promise? You'll try. . . . Okay. I know. . . . I know. Okay. You gotta try, though. . . . Call me when you hear." Doyle huffed and slapped his phone down on the seat between them.

Ryder's head bumped against the glass when they hit a pothole.

"Sorry. Didn't see that." Doyle looked over.

Ryder said, "Two weeks."

"Maybe three." Doyle's voice dripped with hope and

123

goodwill. "Positive thoughts, right?"

"What about Thomas Trent?" The question had been building up inside Ryder since they'd left his mother's hospital room.

"I have no idea."

"You said before that it was a long shot," Ryder said.

Doyle pulled the truck up alongside a fire hydrant beside Ryder's building. "Ryder, you don't even know if this guy is really your dad. You go off and get yourself in all kinds of hot water trying to get into Yankee Stadium."

"I was robbed and then I was desperate." Ryder felt his blood start to boil. "If he *is* my dad, that's not even a lot of money for him. He makes that in a *week*."

Doyle stroked his mustache. "I don't know. It *might* work."

"Because you can't raise the money." Ryder's words came out sounding meaner than he meant them to.

"I *can*. I know I *can*. It's just the *timing*, see? Two weeks, I mean, it's gonna take me that just to fight these guys about the name. Crap!" Doyle slammed his palm against the steering wheel. "Sorry. I shouldn't have said that."

"I've heard lots worse." Ryder stared at the street, the cars and people passing with no idea that his mom was going to die.

"We should try this." Doyle perked up. "You never know which path will lead to success, so you try them all."

"Did you make that up?" Ryder asked.

"No. Read it in one of those books, but it stuck with me. Come on. Let's go get you some clean clothes. You're starting to smell like my dog."

"You got a dog?"

"Brutus. He's a Dalmatian. I'm a fireman, right? We should

124

pop in on Mr. Happy, I mean Mr. Starr. He might have some other ideas on contacting Thomas Trent. Maybe through the team or his agent or something. Maybe he could use the wheelchair bit to get some access. You know, play on their sympathies?"

Ryder followed Doyle out of the truck. He looked at the fire hydrant, but Doyle marched right past without noticing. They mounted the stairs and were huffing by the time they reached the top. Doyle stopped in front of Mr. Starr's door.

"You better not say that stuff about the wheelchair," Ryder warned.

"Oh, he can insult me, but I gotta tickle his ear because he's in a chair?" Doyle wrinkled his face. "Give me a break. The guy's a crab. I don't care if he's in a chair or has a gold medal for winning the hundred-meter dash. I treat everyone the same."

Doyle knocked, loud.

"Leave me alone!" Mr. Starr screamed even louder, enough for Ryder to wince and cover his ears. "I told you, there's no Stephen Starr here!"

Doyle shook his head and shouted through the door. "It's *us*!"

The chair whirred from within, coming closer and closer until it stopped and the lock rattled. The door swung open, banged Mr. Starr's chair, and shut again.

"Stupid door!" Mr. Starr pulled it open again, hooking it with a claw and glaring up at them. "So, they let you loose?"

They followed him into the living room. The chair spun around suddenly. "Armed robbery? You had a knife?"

"No." Ryder shook his head violently at the craziness of the story. "It wasn't me."

"Didn't think so." Mr. Starr glared at Doyle. "The incompetence of these government workers never ceases to astound me."

"See?" Doyle looked at Ryder.

Ryder sat on the edge of the couch along with Doyle and told Mr. Starr everything that happened.

Mr. Starr's eyes widened and softened as he heard the part about Doyle rescuing him from a foster home, or worse.

Ryder finished with the part about his mom and the doctor's report.

"Well, the fireman is right about one thing." Mr. Starr's head seemed to tremble. "We need to try."

"See?" Doyle nudged Ryder. "I'm right."

"But you're wrong about another thing. A big one." Mr. Starr seemed almost pleased.

"What's that?"

## 36

"You can't save her with your fireman's fund scheme. You'll never get that done." Mr. Starr spoke with unwavering certainty.

Doyle seemed nervous, and when his phone played a tune, he yanked it from his pocket like it was on fire. "Hello? Yeah, I know. I *know* I'm on duty. Where? At the neighbor's with the kid."

Doyle listened and his mustache quivered before he grunted and hung up. "That was Derek. Social services isn't happy with the judge's ruling. They're investigating my relationship with Ryder. Guess they spoke to the school and decided you aren't going to fit the bill as a guardian."

"Meaning?" Mr. Starr asked the question Ryder wanted to ask, but was afraid to hear the answer.

"Derek's holding them off down at the station, but they

want to talk to the chief." Doyle pounded a fist into his open hand and gave Ryder a grim look. "After they do that, odds are they're going to take you away."

Ryder stared hard at Doyle. "Is Mr. Starr right? You can't raise the money? In time?"

"I . . ." Doyle's mouth stayed open, but no more words came out.

"Would you bet her life on it?" Ryder asked quietly. "Two hundred thousand dollars?"

Ryder watched Doyle's face turn red. "I can't promise. No."

"So, that makes it easy," Ryder said.

Mr. Starr narrowed his eyes. "Easy?"

"Yes." Ryder had never been more certain of anything in his life. "Now we know there's only one thing we can do. We're going to Atlanta."

# 37

"*I* can't go to Atlanta." Doyle pointed to his own chest. "Then I really *will* lose my job."

"Who said you?" Ryder asked.

"Well, not *you*." Doyle huffed.

"Not *just* me." Ryder put a thumb in his own chest before pointing. "Me and Mr. Starr."

"Him?" Doyle wrinkled his brow.

"I don't think I can do this without a grown-up," Ryder said. "Mr. Starr is the best choice anyway. He used to be a crime reporter. An *investigative* reporter."

Mr. Starr's face glowed.

"Yeah, but . . . how can you get around?" Doyle threw his hands in the air.

"I think disabled people can go anyplace they want to," Ryder said.

Mr. Starr wheeled the chair toward his bedroom without comment, motor humming. "Come on, Ryder. Help me pack."

Ryder glanced at Doyle, who seemed totally flustered, and then he followed Mr. Starr into his bedroom. Mr. Starr instructed Ryder where to find a duffel bag in the closet and then had him pull the dresser drawers open one at a time to transfer certain clothes into the bag.

Doyle appeared and leaned in the doorway with a frown. "And what? You'll just wheel that thing up to Thomas Trent's front door?"

"If we have to." Ryder stuffed four pairs of socks into the bag.

"I really can't go." Doyle stroked his mustache.

Mr. Starr cranked his chair a quarter turn to look at the fireman. "We don't need you to go, Doyle."

"You called me Doyle." Doyle tilted his head. "And you don't sound crabby. Don't try and guilt me into this."

"I'm being serious," Mr. Starr said. "Ryder's right. We can do this, and, if you go meet the social services people at your fire station, we know we'll have time to make our escape. You're the distraction. I won't call you live bait."

"But . . ." Doyle didn't finish.

Mr. Starr raised a crooked hand, extending a single finger in the air. "Ryder's right. He and I can do this. A kid with a sick old man in a wheelchair? That's as good a formula for getting to meet a sports star as anything. Not even a fireman can beat a wheelchair-bound old man and a kid."

Doyle grinned and nodded and Ryder knew it was because that was exactly what Doyle was saying in the truck outside.

Ryder felt better that the two adults in his life right now agreed. It gave him hope.

"Do you need some money?" Doyle asked.

Ryder looked to Mr. Starr. "Do we?"

"No, but thank you. I have a credit card with a big limit because I always pay my bills on time," Mr. Starr said.

"Can you fly on a plane in . . . your condition?" Doyle asked.

"No. But we can take a train. The Crescent line goes from New York to Atlanta every morning." Mr. Starr advanced his chair with a little leap toward Doyle as if to challenge him. "Do you think you can keep the social services people at bay for twelve hours or so?"

"I think I can throw them off your trail." Doyle grinned.

"Yes, fortunately," Mr. Starr said, "like most civil servants, they're not apt to be that bright."

"There he goes again." Doyle threw his hands up and gave Ryder a disgusted look. "Just when I think we're on the same team."

"We are on the same team, but for every star a team has, they've also got a bunch of third-string substitutes." Mr. Starr stared without blinking.

"And *I'm* supposed to be third string?" Doyle shook his head. "I've heard it all now."

"Get going, already," Mr. Starr said. "Everyone has their role. Tell us if we're going to have to rush out of here and spend the night in Penn Station. If we don't hear from you, we'll assume we can get a good night's sleep before our trip."

Doyle reached over Mr. Starr and handed Ryder a card he'd

taken from his wallet. "I'll be on duty until after you two take off. All my information is on this. You call me when you get there, okay?"

Ryder pocketed the card and nodded. "Please check in on my mom." He took a deep breath. "And tell me if there's any change."

Doyle nodded and squeezed past the chair and started down the stairs.

As the footsteps faded, Ryder suddenly felt uncertain about their plan. He looked at Mr. Starr, bent and twisted in his chair, practically helpless. Then, he looked down at his own twelve-year-old arms and legs and wondered if going without Doyle was a huge mistake.

# 38

Amy Gillory had switched her schedule and arrived in the morning. Neither Ryder nor Mr. Starr acted like anything was out of sorts. The Crescent train left Penn Station in the afternoon. When the nurse had gone, Ryder filled a duffel bag with clean clothes and his toothbrush and some toothpaste. He also took some snacks from the kitchen.

"You have the signed ball, right?" Mr. Starr had already packed his own things and had wheeled himself into Ryder's living room.

Ryder dug it out of his pocket. "I never let go of it."

"I'm glad you have it," Mr. Starr said. "I think it's our silver bullet."

"Isn't that to kill monsters with?" Ryder asked. "A silver bullet?"

Mr. Starr puckered his lips. "I suppose, but it's a saying that means like your secret weapon. Something to get the job done in a big way."

Ryder picked the TracFone up off the kitchen table.

"I think I may need you to dial Ashleigh Love for me," Mr. Starr said as Ryder slipped the phone in his pocket.

"Your other nurse? Do you need her?" Ryder held up the phone.

Mr. Starr's face reddened a bit. "If we're going to be gone for a few days, I do need her to make some adjustments for me, yes."

"Will she try to stop you?"

"She might try and talk me out of it," Mr. Starr said. "But she'll do what I ask. She's too kind not to."

"Is this . . . are you going to . . . are you okay to do this?" Ryder asked.

"Do we have a choice?"

"Mr. Starr, I . . ."

"I'll be fine." Mr. Starr sounded mean again. "Just dial the girl, will you? 917-555-6344."

Ryder dialed and held the phone up to Mr. Starr's ear. He could hear Ashleigh Love's voice. She did ask him not to go and Ryder got to hear all about how he needed his therapy on a daily basis to keep the blood flowing through his body and keep him from getting sick. In the end, she agreed to meet them between jobs at the train station and get Mr. Starr fixed up as best she could for the trip.

"If you're gone more than a week, you'll have to see some-one down there," Ashleigh said.

"I know that," Mr. Starr snapped. "We'll see you at the

station, next to the Starbucks. I'll buy you a latte."

Ryder hung up and stuffed the phone in his pocket.

"Well, you might as well start wheeling this thing. It'll save the battery. Take me to the service elevator and we'll hope the super has stayed sober enough to keep at least one thing around here working right. It's the reason the state let me stay in this godforsaken dump—that elevator, and the fact that I know for certain the landlord gets an extra three hundred a month from Social Security because of it."

Ryder grabbed hold of the handles sticking out from the back of the chair and put his weight behind it, surprised at how easily it moved and nearly ramming Mr. Starr into the wall.

"Easy!" Mr. Starr barked.

"Sorry." Ryder backed up, but too fast so that he bumped into a table next to his mother's reading chair. The porcelain lamp wobbled and fell in slow motion. Ryder grabbed for the shade, but the base swung into the wall, smashing into twenty pieces.

"Oh my God." Ryder stared at the blue-and-white shards and what was left of the lamp. "It's her favorite lamp."

"Things break," Mr. Starr said. "Come on. Leave it. We've got a train to catch."

Ryder did as he was told and walked away, uncertain, from the mess. Carefully, he eased Mr. Starr out of the apartment, then up the hallway, turning right toward the lift. They passed several apartments with no tenants because of water damage so severe that the floor had supposedly rotted clean through. Ryder had always been forbidden from the area. His mom said it was dangerous. At the end of the hall Ryder could see where an original wall had been torn down, exposing the service area and the elevator's wide metal doors. On the metal frame was a round button.

"You gotta pound on it to get it to work," Mr. Starr said.

Ryder made a fist and thumped the button. Nothing happened.

"Harder." Mr. Starr sounded impatient.

Ryder struck it again.

"You gotta hit it like five or six times, real hard," Mr. Starr said.

Ryder pounded on it until a little yellow light went on and he could hear the gears and cables working behind the doors. When the elevator arrived and the doors swung open, its floor was a good six inches below where Ryder stood. He looked at Mr. Starr for direction.

"You gotta back me in."

Ryder did, and when the chair banged down onto the elevator floor, Mr. Starr only said, "Good."

Ryder pushed the button for the first floor. The door shut, the elevator jerked, then dropped as if the cable had snapped. As they plummeted down, Ryder could only think of his mom and that he was going to beat her to heaven by two or three weeks.

## 39

The elevator banged and stopped, dashing Ryder to the floor, then rattled and bumped and started to go down again, smoothly this time.

Mr. Starr laughed. "One day it'll snap. When we get back from this, I'll have to remember to put you and your mom in my will. You can sue the landlord and the city for wrongful death. They know this thing is ready to go."

"You should have told me." Ryder couldn't help being angry.

"Why?" Mr. Starr chuckled.

Ryder couldn't think why exactly, because if he was being honest, he'd risk his own life to save his mom's anyway. He knew that. After all, it was just the two of them against the world, and the thought of it made him grit his teeth.

The elevator stopped and opened smoothly with an innocent little ding, as if it hadn't just tried to kill them. Mr. Starr directed him to the back door, where a ramp had been cobbled together out of warped and graying plywood sheets and two-by-four boards. The wood bowed and crackled as Ryder rolled the chair down the ramp and he began to feel less safe than he had on the elevator, but they reached the safety of the alleyway and started on toward the subway.

The elevator in the subway smelled like stale pee. Ryder tried not to breathe through his nose and when the doors finally opened, he'd never felt so relieved to inhale the stale funky air off the subway tunnel. They rode to Penn Station on the C line. On board the subway, Ryder watched the horror flash across people's faces at the sight of Mr. Starr and he burned with shame as they looked quickly away, keeping their eyes off of him as if the sight would turn them to stone. One woman covered her little boy's face and hurried him away, into the next car. Ryder tried not to notice, but it was so obvious that he suspected he knew why Mr. Starr was so bitter.

Out on the street, it hadn't been so bad. He'd been aware of the looks, but people were moving and so were he and Mr. Starr, so he'd been able to ignore it. Here, though, crowded and locked into the rumbling metal tube, there was no escape. Ryder looked around, then let his hands slip from the chair's grips. Slowly and artfully, he moved half a step away, as if he wasn't with Mr. Starr. From his new spot he could see the twisted side of Mr. Starr's cheek and the unblinking eyeball staring straight ahead. Ryder was horrified to be there, but even more horrified with himself for disowning the man who was doing all this for him.

At Columbus Circle, two older teenage boys with long

hair and wearing crested blazers got on, but didn't look away. Instead, they stared at Mr. Starr and nudged each other with their backpacks, giggling and groaning and making horrible frozen faces of their own until they burst out laughing. Ryder boiled. There was nothing he could say, but he took hold of the chair again. He sputtered trying to come up with the right words, but none came and now the boys began to laugh at him, stuttering and pointing.

Without thinking, Ryder sprang across the subway car and poked a finger into the chest of the taller boy, stabbing it into his flesh just below the crest on the jacket pocket like a dagger. "What do you think you're staring at?!"

The boy jumped back with a yell and made a fist.

Ryder made two and his eyes blurred with fury.

## 40

"What's *wrong* with you, dude?" The whine in the older boy's voice told Ryder he had the upper hand.

"You think something's funny?" Ryder snarled. These boys were older and bigger than Ryder, but he wasn't thinking. He was on fire. "Just shut your face!"

The second boy stepped back, slipping into the crowd of people like a mouse desperate for its hole. The taller boy's red face turned purple. "You're a loon, you and Frankenstein. I'll call the cops!"

"Good. Call them." Ryder took another step and shook a fist, still burning and really wanting a fight. The older boy jumped and squirmed back into the crowd like his friend, running and shouting about calling the cops as he made his way to the other end of the car.

Ryder looked around. Everyone stared. His brain cooled.

He let his fists drop and returned to the back of the chair where no one would look. The subway stopped and Ryder's heart galloped at the sight of the two boys in blazers rushing off toward a transit cop and pointing back his way. The cop looked over and widened his eyes at the sight of Mr. Starr, before looking up. Ryder met the cop's eyes without blinking. The cop said something to the boys and shrugged and the subway doors hissed shut and they continued on to Penn Station.

Finally, Mr. Starr spoke in a bored voice. "If you fight everyone who gets a laugh out of my face, we'll never get to Atlanta."

"They . . ." A single angry flame burst to life inside Ryder and he clenched his fists again. "Jerks."

"Ruby's son for sure," Mr. Starr said.

"Why do you say that?" Curiosity doused the flame.

"When she first came to the building, every guy under the age of eighty was interested in her. There was this punk on the second floor who sold pot on the corner. Thought he was a player. He comes by your apartment. You were a baby. I hear shouting and came out—I still could get around back then on crutches. Saw your mom hit that guy with a frying pan. Ha!" Mr. Starr barked and people in the subway glanced at him, then quickly looked away. "I thought that was only in cartoons. Had a lump on his head like a pineapple."

"I never saw her do anything like that," Ryder said. "She takes deep breaths and counts to ten."

"Did you ever step in dog poop?" Mr. Starr asked.

Ryder wrinkled his nose. "What's that got to do with it?"

"Do you stop and put your fist in the pile you just stepped in?" Mr. Starr sounded like he was enjoying himself.

141

"No. That's gross."

"What do you do?"

"Wipe it off?" Ryder said.

"With your fingers?"

Ryder's mouth twisted into a frown. "No. On the grass."

"Right," Mr. Starr said. "You keep walking to get away from the smell and you wipe it off on the grass as you go."

Ryder thought about what he was saying. "Yeah, okay. I get it. Those idiots are dog poop."

"I'm serious." Mr. Starr did sound serious now. "Do not do that again."

"But . . ."

"I mean it, Ryder. You're not helping anyone." Then his voice softened. "I appreciate that you tried to defend me, and I was half hoping you'd bust him right in the mouth. But please, if I have to be defended by a twelve-year-old boy, how do you think that makes me feel?"

Ryder shrugged, trying to understand. He gripped the handles on the wheelchair tight and glared at anyone who tried to sneak peeks at Mr. Starr as they rode along.

When they arrived at Penn Station, Mr. Starr directed him to the Starbucks. Ashleigh Love stood waiting for them with a satiny blue Yankees jacket over her nurse's uniform. She had a small duffel bag of supplies over her shoulder and wore a worried look on her face. She immediately took control of the chair from Ryder, heading toward the handicap bathroom as she chided Mr. Starr for his crazy idea.

"You can't just *go* to Atlanta," she said. "You've got to have therapy and you've got to stay clean. You'll get an infection and then you'll be in the hospital."

They reached the handicap bathroom. Ryder opened the door and in they went while Ryder stayed behind, closing the door on the sound of Ashleigh Love, a buzz now as she continued to tell Mr. Starr why he shouldn't go. Ryder looked up at the big board listing the trains and found the one for Atlanta as the voices hummed back and forth from inside the bathroom.

He had no idea what they were saying, but when Ryder heard Mr. Starr suddenly shriek at her with a sound that punched right through the metal door, he stepped away. Ryder found a bench and sat down. He pulled the baseball out of his pocket, and wondered where Thomas Trent had given it to his mother. Were they out at a movie? Dinner? Maybe on a picnic blanket on some lazy summer day.

Ryder had plenty of those kinds of days together with his mom in Central Park at the Strawberry Fields. They'd spread their blanket, eat sandwiches, read books, toss a Frisbee. Then one day—Ryder was probably seven—a baseball rolled onto their blanket. Before the boys who'd been playing catch could get there, Ryder picked up the ball. He could still remember how right it felt in his hand, the perfect size, the perfect weight, and those wonderful red stitches.

He chucked that ball right back to one of the boys, surprising everyone when that ball snapped back into the boy's glove like a gunshot.

"Wow." The boy addressed Ryder's mom. "Is that your little brother?"

Ryder's mom smiled. "No, he's my son."

"Well, hey," the kid said, "you oughta sign him up."

His mother laughed. "No, he's going to be a doctor, not a baseball player."

"Well, with an arm like that, he could be both, right?" The boys laughed pleasantly and went back to their game of catch, but the words were locked in Ryder's head.

From that moment, Ryder pestered his mom endlessly for baseballs and mitts and bats and to sign him up for Little League. Finally, two years later, she gave in. He'd never forget that moment either. It was the last night of sign-ups at the school.

They sat reading together, but he'd only spoken to her in single-word replies since dinner.

She slapped her book down on the lamp table and stood up abruptly. "Oh, I can't stand it already. Get your coat."

"Where?" Ryder asked.

"I'll sign you up, but you better get all As. One B, and it's over. Deal?"

Ryder grinned. "Deal."

The bargain worked for both of them, but he could never figure why she'd always been reluctant about baseball. Even when she couldn't contain her pride when he outshone all the other boys in a game, there was always something sad about her face, a smile that melted too quickly, laughter cut short by a faraway look.

The thought of that day in the park when that ball rolled onto their blanket made Ryder choke. He looked around the train station at the tide of people, coming and going, and shook his head at the craziness of his life, wishing he'd only not been so cheeky with his mom and stopped in his tracks, just to aggravate her. Then he wouldn't be sitting in the middle of Penn Station, waiting to ride a train halfway across the country to try and find a man who might not even be his father.

# 41

Mr. Starr came out of the bathroom with Ashleigh pushing the chair. Ryder tucked the baseball away and they walked silently to Track 8. Ashleigh helped them board and get situated in their sleeper car. She took a white paper bag from her duffel and handed it to Ryder. Inside were some bananas and sandwiches and two bottles of water.

She looked at Ryder. "You'll have to feed him, you know."

"I figured. It's no big deal." Ryder tried not to look at Mr. Starr, but he felt those eyes on him and it made his face warm.

Ashleigh shook her head, then gave Mr. Starr a kiss on the cheek. "You be careful."

"I promise not to run around on the train," Mr. Starr said.

She smiled and shook her head one final time and left them.

Ryder looked at Mr. Starr from his seat on the edge of the bed. The train began to move, slowly gaining speed. He knew they were going down, through a tunnel under the Hudson River. It was amazing and as they went Ryder marveled at the things people could do. Suddenly, they emerged into the light of day.

"Okay, get the iPad," Mr. Starr said, as if he'd only been waiting for them to officially leave New York.

Ryder got the tablet out of Mr. Starr's bag and turned it on. Mr. Starr instructed him on how to link up to the train's Wi-Fi and soon Ryder was looking at the Google home page.

"In 1997 four young girls were strangled in Harlem." Mr. Starr's eyes lost their focus as he stared out the window.

Electric poles shot past, ticking away the distance, and Ryder looked at Mr. Starr curiously.

"It didn't get too much attention," Mr. Starr said, "because the politicians and the police didn't want people getting excited. New York was being marketed as a safe city and, after all, to them it was just Harlem. The cops were getting nowhere. Then I got the case to investigate for the newspaper. I did all this research, interviews. And I found him, a complete maniac. He was a pharmacist, with two little girls of his own, a town house out near the Throgs Neck Bridge. Unbelievable, but I found him."

Mr. Starr locked his eyes on Ryder. "I'm trying to say that I know what I'm doing. We've got a good eighteen hours and the internet. We need to get inside Thomas Trent's world, and we will."

"Are we going to write another note?" Ryder asked.

"I don't think we have time anymore to see if he reacts to a note," Mr. Starr said. "I think you're going to have to press him on the spot."

"Press him?"

"Tell him you're his son, tell him your mom needs his help, that he has to save her life. I know it's going to be hard, but you're going to have to do it, Ryder."

Ryder nodded his head. He understood.

They worked all day and long into the night before Ryder helped Mr. Starr eat his sandwich, then get into the bathroom, then into the lower bunk. Ryder used the bathroom himself, then climbed up into the top bunk without a word. The train rattled and shook and clapped the rails, heaving them about in their beds. Ryder reached for his coat to use as padding to keep his head from banging the wall. He folded it, felt the lump, then unfolded it and dug into the pocket, removing the baseball, which he held in one hand.

They rode through a small town with streetlights that flashed past, casting their strobe on the ball. The squiggle of ink they believed to be Thomas Trent's signature appeared and disappeared. The words RUBY and GEM jumped out at him, making him want to laugh and cry at the same time.

He remembered another man who loved Ruby, or Ryder presumed he had. Ryder had been so young that the man was one of his earliest memories. The man was always nice to Ryder, but he didn't act like other people, didn't laugh when you should, or yell when you should do that. He wore a long tan camel hair coat with dark brown gloves and shoes that reflected the light. Beneath his overcoat were suits so soft, Ryder liked to simply touch his arm. The ties around his neck were rich in color, knotted crisply against stiff-collared shirts. The watch on his wrist was gold with sparkling diamonds on its face.

Ryder's mom would make dinner for them all and the man always ate with easy manners that made him seem warm as well as rich. The man wanted to take Ruby away. Ryder heard him say so. He wanted Ryder to go to a boarding school. Ryder heard that too with his ear pressed close to the crack in their bedroom door. Then he heard his mother yelling and the man never returned. Ryder never asked about the man, but he thought about him as he grew older and understood what it was really all about.

The train clacked and Ryder sniffed back some tears, trying to think positive thoughts. There were—after all—men in the world who *could* save his mother, save her still.

They left the lights of the town and everything was so dark he could no longer see the words on the baseball, but only feel the rough dry seams and the solid mass, something so dense and unbreakable that it might be the core of a future planet.

Ryder sighed and held the ball next to his cheek. As he dropped into sleep he allowed the image of Thomas Trent to spring up in his mind, heroic and strong and ready to save them all.

## 42

Ryder slept poorly and when he woke for good, the smell of diesel and the motion of the train left him feeling queasy. He found his baseball and, clutching it, hung over the edge of the bunk to see Mr. Starr lying in the bottom bunk with eyes wide open.

"You're up. Good. Help me into the bathroom." Mr. Starr sounded annoyed and Ryder wondered why he didn't just wake him up if he was going to be mad about Ryder sleeping.

Ryder climbed down, stuffing the baseball into his duffel bag, and helped him into the bathroom. He tried hard not to hear any of the noises being made.

At the sound of the flush, Ryder paused, then asked if he should open the door. Mr. Starr said he should and he did.

"Thank you." Mr. Starr's voice barely slipped free from his mouth, so Ryder didn't reply. "Help me into the chair."

Ryder did.

"Now," Mr. Starr said, using his eyes to direct Ryder, "take the credit card and get us some breakfast. A muffin and coffee for me. Get yourself whatever you like."

Ryder nodded and left. He came back a few minutes later, and fed Mr. Starr a muffin and coffee, bringing things to his lips as carefully as he could with the rocking train. When he was done, Ryder took a few moments to eat his own egg sandwich.

"Nice work," Mr. Starr said when they'd finished. "Now, back to Thomas Trent. I was thinking about everything we know. The Braves don't play until tomorrow. They have batting practice later today, though. If we can get out to the stadium, we might get the chance to see him coming out of the players' parking lot."

They knew from their research that Thomas Trent drove a dark blue Maserati.

"If we miss him there today, we'll try the dugout at the game tomorrow, because as much as I'd like to ambush him in his driveway at home, we'll never get into the development."

"I don't want to go there anyway." Ryder frowned at the thought.

Thomas Trent, like many of the professional athletes and music stars in Atlanta, lived in a gated neighborhood of mansions called Country Club of the South. On the internet, Mr. Starr had actually been able to bring up an image of the place Thomas Trent lived in with his wife and two young children. It made Ryder's heart swell with envy—the tall white columns, the neatly trimmed hedges and trees, and the numerous rows of wide windows. The place looked more like a courthouse than a home and Ryder could only imagine what it looked like on the inside, maybe a five-star hotel like the one whose bathrooms his mother cleaned.

Ryder also knew—from their research—exactly how much money his father made. Twelve million dollars a year. It staggered him to even think about, but it also filled him with hope because, after all, for someone who made that much money, what was two hundred thousand? Pocket change.

"I'm glad you said that," Mr. Starr said.

"What?" Ryder realized Mr. Starr's eyes were on him, digging into his mind.

"That you don't want to go there," Mr. Starr said. "I think our best chance for success will be the kind of deal that leaves everything just the way it is for Trent."

"What do you mean?" Ryder studied those eyes.

## 43

Mr. Starr sighed. "A lot of people might look at this as some kind of winning lottery ticket."

"If he pays for my mom's operation, that's the only ticket I need," Ryder said.

"You looked at the pictures of that house for a long time is all I'm saying," Mr. Starr said. "And I saw your lips moving when you added up the salaries he's made in the last ten years."

"Only because I'm thinking how easy this will be for him if he has any kind of a heart at all. What? Why are you looking at me like that?" Ryder asked.

"I think Cinderella has been around for a long time because people ache for a fairy godmother," Mr. Starr said, "someone to solve *all* their problems, not just one."

The train wobbled and jerked as they pulled into the station, then slowed to a stop. Ryder slung the duffel bags over the back of the wheelchair and backed Mr. Starr out of their compartment. The doors hissed open and Ryder was on his way, wheeling Mr. Starr through the station toward the MARTA trains before he spoke again.

"I don't even like this guy," Ryder said.

"Don't say that." Mr. Starr had obviously been waiting for him to resume the discussion. "You don't know him."

"I know he left me and my mom." Ryder had forgotten about the stares in the subway, but now that they were out in the open again, people were gawking at Mr. Starr.

"No," Mr. Starr said, "you don't. Your mom may have left him."

"Right. Seriously?" Ryder forced himself to ignore the passing stares.

"Don't think that what people do always makes sense. Also, I've learned that just when you think you know exactly what happened to someone, you're surprised by the fact that the opposite of what you think is the truth. We'll have to buy MARTA passes. See those ticket windows over there?"

"Yes. I don't even want to talk about it."

"Neither do I," Mr. Starr said. "I just want your mind to be in the right place when we get to meet him because you won't get another chance at this. You have to know what you want from him and what you don't. If you want a fairy godmother, he's apt to tell you to call his lawyer and you'll never see him again. No matter what happened between him and your mom—and listen, I've got to say this, maybe nothing at all happened, we don't *know* he's your father—he's going to want to keep the life he has. That's part of what could help us here. But in a way, this is sort of blackmail."

"Blackmail?" Ryder stopped pushing the chair and he moved around front so he could see Mr. Starr's eyes. "What are you talking about? I'm not expecting my dad to all of a sudden be a part of my life—toss a baseball around or go for a bike ride. That's not what this is about. It's about my mom. We're asking him to help someone whose life he and I destroyed."

"Destroyed?" Mr. Starr blinked and his voice turned soft. "Ryder, is that what you think you did to her?"

Suddenly, Ryder felt tears in his eyes, remembering the man in the camel hair coat, and he barked at Mr. Starr. "Look at her. She's wonderful. She's beautiful. And she spends her life cleaning toilets because of *me*. She could walk down Park Avenue and have some rich guy with a limo wanting to marry her before she went five blocks, but she *can't* because she's got *me*."

"She does have you." Mr. Starr kept his voice soft but strong, and he sat like an immovable rock in the tide of people washing in and out and around them in the station. "And look where you are. Look what you've done already to try and save her. She has a knight for a son, a warrior."

Ryder had to laugh, and he sniffed and looked away, embarrassed that he'd actually thought of himself as a knight already.

"I'm serious. You're fighting to save her. Look at what you've been through already. I know you're only twelve, but you're Odysseus. This is your odyssey. She loves you, Ryder, and she should. Go ahead. Get two three-day train passes."

"Three days?" Ryder asked.

"Let's hope that's all it takes. I have the feeling it'll be more, but when one can be optimistic and frugal in the same moment, one always should." Mr. Starr's eyes sparkled. "I think I'd write that down if I could write. Go ahead. Get the tickets. We just might make it to the stadium before the players all go home."

With the passes in hand, the two of them loaded onto a MARTA train headed for the Five Points station. From Five Points, they transferred to a bus that took them to the stadium. Mr. Starr kept fretting about the time, but finally, they got off in front of the stadium, the lift hissing and groaning as it delivered the wheelchair to the curb. The stares from other passengers annoyed Ryder more than they embarrassed him, and he considered that progress. The bus roared away, leaving them to choke on its diesel fumes. The sidewalks were mostly empty and the banners hung limp from the stadium ramparts.

Ryder shielded his eyes against the bright sky and studied the walls rising straight from the ground. A massive bronze statue of Hank Aaron towered over them.

"We have to go around to the back." Mr. Starr sounded annoyed. "Hurry up. They're probably done with practice by now."

Ryder took hold of the chair and started to push, rounding the stadium like an ancient knight at a siege, circling the fortress, preventing any escape.

"Faster."

Ryder pumped his legs. They hit a groove in the walkway. The wheelchair jounced and Mr. Starr grunted in pain. Ryder slowed.

"Go!" Mr. Starr's shriek echoed off the stadium's brick wall and back into the wide street crawling with cars.

"Are you okay?" Ryder was losing his breath with the effort.

"Go!"

Ryder winced and surged ahead, huffing. He could see the corner of the stadium now.

"Left at the light," Mr. Starr commanded.

Ryder took the corner fast, nearly spilling Mr. Starr into the street. He kept everything upright, but now his biggest problem wasn't to push, it was to pull. The sidewalk plunged down through two columns of trees, with the media entrance on the left. Pulling and hurrying at the same time, they passed the media gate, then an entrance for the police where only a single uniformed officer stood drinking coffee. The sidewalk flattened out. A fence appeared on the left. Through the slats Ryder spied the expensive cars in the players' parking lot.

Ahead was the opening to the players' lot, barred by a huge metal gate and a security shack. Even though it was only a practice day, a small crowd of crazed fans stood like street people, clustered at the mouth of the opening. A big black SUV, a Cadillac Escalade with glinting chrome, rolled out through the gate and kept on going past the hopeful fans waving their pennants, gloves, cards, bats, and baseballs to be signed. Two security guards in bright yellow jackets held up their arms and pushed the crowd back so the SUV could pass.

"Hurry!"

Ryder huffed and searched for a pocket of energy. Part of him wondered why Mr. Starr was so urgent, until they reached the opening and he saw the long blue Maserati rolling up on the inside of the gate, nearly upon them. Ryder could barely breathe, let alone signal to Thomas Trent. In that instant, he saw the pitcher's face through the windshield and the blank stare painted darker still by the fancy sunglasses hiding his eyes.

"Go!"

"Mr. Starr?"

Ryder had no idea what he was expected to do. The car was coming and it wasn't slowing down. Thomas Trent, like the player before him, had finished practice and was heading home to his family, in no mood to stop for a small pack of rabid fans. There'd be time for them tomorrow, at the game.

One of the guards had slicked-back hair and when he saw them, he shouted, "Hey! Get back!"

Mr. Starr roared. "I said 'Go'! Stop him! Push me! Stop him!"

Ryder pulled up short, but the chair kept going. Mr. Starr had his crooked hand on the control, jamming it forward. The chair lurched ahead. Ryder leapt for the chair, grabbing for the handles to restrain Mr. Starr—trying to save his life.

The Maserati swerved and blared its horn.

# 44

Something hit Ryder from the side. He fell and his hold on the chair spun it sideways, tipping it over. The side of Ryder's head struck the pavement and he saw stars that blurred his vision. He felt a great weight on top of him and realized he'd been buried under Mr. Starr and the chair. Mr. Starr flopped and wriggled and bellowed.

Ryder's head cleared as the security guards righted the chair and lifted Mr. Starr up before lowering him into his seat. The small crowd all backed off, wide-eyed and muttering to each other about the crazy kid and the messed-up guy in the chair. Ryder's face flushed.

He glanced around and realized the Maserati had disappeared. He felt a stab of bitter resentment in his heart. What kind of a man could nearly run over an old man in a wheelchair and then drive off without a backward glance?

"What's wrong with you, kid?" The guard with dark, slicked-back hair was in Ryder's face; his black sunglasses were steamed around the edges and his breath was hot. "You can't do that. You're lucky nobody got hurt."

Ryder rubbed the side of his head, wincing at the tender bump.

"You two are lucky I don't call the cops!" Mr. Starr's frozen face was red and sweaty and his voice had an edge like broken glass.

The other security guard took a radio off his belt and held it up to Mr. Starr. "You want the police? I can call them right now and we can make sure you two get to see the judge so we can get a restraining order against you. How'd you like that? You try to purposely stop a player just for an autograph? I can put an end to any autographs for you. You'll be banned from Turner Field for life. So, you want the cops? They're right up the hill."

The guard had a black beard and mustache around just his mouth, and the way he stroked it as he waited for Mr. Starr's answer reminded Ryder of Doyle McDonald. Mr. Starr's eyes smoldered as he considered his options. Ryder knew Mr. Starr was burning with rage and he held his breath, knowing the wrong answer would be the end of everything.

# 45

"My chair." Mr. Starr's voice shook. "The control got stuck. . . . I'm very sorry."

The guard let out a sigh and the hand with the radio dropped to his side. "I'm sorry you fell over. We didn't want you to get hit."

"Thomas Trent wasn't too worried, was he?" Mr. Starr stared at the guard, his eyes as frozen as his body.

The guard shrugged. "I doubt he even saw you fall. He swerved and went the other way. When he slowed down these other people mobbed his car and he kept going. You can't blame him for your stuck control."

"That's right," Mr. Starr said, "but maybe he could give us an autograph tomorrow? You know . . . for the trouble. We came all the way from New York."

"Yeah. You talk like a New Yorker. Tomorrow?" The guard

nodded and gave his partner a quick look. "Sure. You come back tomorrow and we'll work something out. I'll talk to Mr. Trent and see if he wouldn't mind. Sound good?"

Mr. Starr's eyes gleamed. "Very good. Thanks. Ryder, let's go. Back the way we came."

Another shiny SUV—a pearl Range Rover—pulled up and out through the opening. The crowd came back to life, hopeful and unified as a school of fish flashing in the sun even as the player kept on going. Ryder turned the chair and headed away, expecting Mr. Starr to direct him back to the bus stop. He was pleasantly surprised when he told him to cross at the light toward the Country Inn & Suites on the other side.

"The perfect place for a bivouac," Mr. Starr said.

"A what?"

"Don't they teach you anything in these schools?" Mr. Starr said with disgust in his voice. "A biv-o-wack is a military encampment, only usually it provides very little shelter. This won't be that bad, and from here we plan and launch our campaign."

"Oh, that." Ryder angled his thumb toward the stadium.

"Yes, that. There's a break in the curb for handicap access. I don't need to get thrown out of this thing again, in case you thought I liked the show back there."

"I can't believe he didn't stop." Ryder pushed the chair up to the front doors and they rolled open automatically.

"He doesn't have to be a saint, you know. We're not expecting an invitation to Christmas dinner, remember."

"I know." Ryder shrugged, and noted the horrified facial reaction of the girl behind the reception desk as they approached.

"I'd like to think my father has a little bit of a heart, though."

"We were two crazy strangers in the midst of a bunch of crackpot autograph hounds. I can't blame him for mashing the gas."

"I don't think he mashed the gas," Ryder said.

"How would you know? You were being mashed by me."

Ryder had to laugh, even though his head still hurt. He rubbed the bump. "Yeah, I was."

Mr. Starr turned his attention to the girl behind the desk. He had made a reservation online, and with Ryder's help to dig out his credit card, they got checked in, and Ryder wheeled him into their ground-floor room.

"Get unpacked," Mr. Starr said. "We may be here a while."

"But the security guard said—"

Mr. Starr waved a claw impatiently. "We aren't going to get a check for two hundred thousand dollars along with a free autograph because we announce that you're his son and your mother needs an operation. Tomorrow is just our first point of contact, our opening sortie if we stay with the military theme. This thing will take a few days . . . at least. You can put your clothes in the top drawer."

Ryder unpacked them and then Mr. Starr declared that he was hungry, so Ryder retrieved some pulled pork sandwiches from a place next door called the Bullpen Rib House. After they ate, Mr. Starr announced that they were going to the Georgia Aquarium.

"We are?" Ryder said.

"We have time to kill, and when I was a reporter I got in the habit of seeing the sights whenever I had time to kill. Supposedly, the aquarium here is worth the time and the money. We'll see about that. It's open late, so we're good."

Ryder maneuvered the wheelchair down the sidewalk, across the street, and onto the bus that arrived five minutes later. They headed straight for the golden dome of the capitol building, then wound their way through the heart of Atlanta to Centennial Park. The aquarium was amazing and Ryder appreciated the ease of everything with Mr. Starr being in a wheelchair. They got to cut every line and see everything up as close as you could get. Ryder almost said something about how good it was that Mr. Starr was in a chair, but didn't, and then wondered if he'd lost his own mind when he stopped looking at fish and saw the stares from all around. Ryder realized that no one would trade places with Mr. Starr, not even the poorest, dirtiest, most desperate person on the street. No one wanted to go through life in a chair, and especially in pain.

When they got back to their hotel room and finally shut the door on the gawking faces of other people, Ryder thought about what Mr. Starr was enduring because of him and his mom. "Thank you, Mr. Starr."

"I haven't done anything yet." Mr. Starr sat in his chair, just staring out the window at downtown Atlanta. "Let's hold off until we get the job done."

"Thank you for even trying. My mom and I, we don't get a lot of help from people. We rely on each other all the time. I don't know what I would have done without you."

"You certainly can't hang your hopes on that mangy fireman."

"I like Doyle, Mr. Starr. He helped me a lot too. I'd probably be in a foster home if it wasn't for him."

"Well, yes. We'll have to give him a bit of credit. I suppose his heart is generally in the right place, even if his brain is lagging behind."

Ryder chuckled and shook his head, knowing there wasn't any hope. "Maybe we should call him."

"Not on my dime." Mr. Starr's words dripped with disgust.

"Maybe he got permission to use FDNY to help raise money. We should at least check in, Mr. Starr. I want to see if there's any news on my mom."

Mr. Starr stared for a minute, then cleared his throat. "Here. Get the iPad. Send an email if you must."

"That'll work." Ryder tried not to grin as he started up the iPad and sent Doyle an email asking how his mom was doing and for a progress report as well as giving one of his own. He ended the email with the sentence:

Looks like tomorrow will be a very big day.

He was disappointed that they got no reply from Doyle before the time Mr. Starr said it was time to turn off the TV and for them to get some rest.

"Tomorrow," Mr. Starr said, "*is* a big day, maybe the biggest in your life."

## 46

The next day, the Braves had an afternoon game against the Dodgers with the first pitch set for one o'clock. Ryder and Mr. Starr had breakfast in the dining area just off the hotel lobby, then returned to their room to fuss around with the iPad. They pretended to each other that they needed more information to complete the picture of Thomas Trent's life, but they really had everything necessary, and a lot more to boot. Ryder even found out that Thomas Trent's wife grew up outside of Cleveland, Ohio, as the daughter of a farmer, and got suspended from her high school soccer team for drinking in her senior year.

"Okay," Mr. Starr said after they unearthed that fact. "We've got more than enough."

Just as he spoke, a bell dinged on the iPad signaling an incoming email. It was from Doyle and Ryder nearly panicked as he hurried to open it and scan its contents.

"Well?" Mr. Starr asked. "What's the news?"

Ryder shook his head and dipped his chin. "He didn't get it, the FDNY thing. But my mom's okay. Well, no change anyway."

"That just makes today that much more important."

"Are you trying to make me nervous?" Ryder tried not to sound annoyed, but the magnitude of meeting his father was overwhelming.

"No. I'm trying to help you focus. Let's get ourselves together."

Ryder pulled on a sweatshirt and stuffed his baseball and the Sharpie in the big front pocket. They decided that he'd hand Thomas Trent the ball and pen, asking him to sign it in hopes that the sight of his old double-A signature would add credibility to their story.

Ryder's limbs shook as he eased the wheelchair down the sidewalk through the column of trees toward the players' parking lot. It was nine forty-five and the air still had a chill even though the sun was rising fast and warming things up nicely. The clear blue sky promised an exceptional day for baseball and maybe the beginning of a whole new kind of life for Ryder. He couldn't help secretly wishing for that, despite what he told Mr. Starr.

They weren't the first fans to arrive. A small family with heavy Southern accents grinned and nodded at them. They looked like farmers and they were the first people Ryder had seen who didn't look at Mr. Starr with horror, fascination, or disgust. Ryder took it as yet another sign that this was going to be a good day with things going their way. More fans wandered up who weren't as polite, but at least no one said anything about Mr. Starr. The security guards appeared suddenly from their shack.

"Do you see the ones from yesterday?" Mr. Starr's eyes jumped past the guard who had emerged.

"No," Ryder said.

One of the security guards was scrawny and weather-worn with scraggly blond hair and a mustache, but the other one was enormous.

"Guy looks like a buffalo." Mr. Starr spoke low.

Ryder nodded in agreement. The guard had a shaggy-haired head, no neck, and appeared to weigh at least four hundred pounds. The buffalo guard put his hands on the heavy metal sections of temporary fence that had been put in place over-night to keep people from crossing the driveway and rattled them, as if to test their strength. The skinny guard did the same to the sections across the driveway.

"Excuse me," Mr. Starr said. "Can you help us?"

If either of them heard Mr. Starr, they ignored him and took up their posts at the end of the fences where the driveway met the road.

"Hey!" Mr. Starr shouted. "Hey! I'm talking to *you*!"

The big guard answered Mr. Starr's words with a scowl.

"Yes, you!" Mr. Starr was unfazed. "Where are those meat-heads from yesterday? They promised us an autograph from Thomas Trent. The guy with the slicked-back hair and the little black beard? He said we could come inside the gate."

"I doubt that." The big guard rumbled like distant thunder. "You all just stay right where you are." He stood with his arms folded across his massive chest like he was guarding a bank vault.

"Hey!" Mr. Starr shrieked so loud Ryder winced.

"Maybe we should just ask quietly," Ryder suggested.

"Squeaky wheel gets the grease. Trust me on that." Mr. Starr harrumphed. "I am serious! We were promised! Do you know how hard it is for me to be wheeled around? I know I sound like a grouch, but look at me! You'd be a grouch too! Now, you stop ignoring me! We were promised!"

The skinny guard shot a nervous glance at the big one, but the big buffalo showed no emotion, and when he looked their way, he looked right over Mr. Starr, as if he were nothing more than a fire hydrant.

"Fine." Mr. Starr muttered so low, Ryder didn't know if he intended to be heard. "I'll give them a repeat of yesterday. Let him run me over this time."

"Mr. Starr, *no*." Ryder's voice was hushed and urgent. "Please let's just try. He might stop and sign. If not, we can go inside and try the dugout."

"They lied to us, Ryder. They played us. I can't bear it. Being in this chair gives me an edge and I intend to use it."

"Like yesterday?" Ryder felt panic rising up inside him. "Please, Mr. Starr. We should be low-key about this. I don't want to start things off bad. I want to make a good impression."

"He's a pro ballplayer, for God's sake." Mr. Starr clucked his tongue. "If anyone understands determination, it'll be a pro ballplayer. The squeaky wheel, Ryder. The squeaky wheel wins, even if it's uncomfortable, the squeaky wheel gets the grease. It's human nature. I've seen it over and over again."

Mr. Starr got hold of his control and backed his chair away from the driveway, nearly running over a little girl with her father.

"Where are you going?" Ryder hurried to keep up, worried that they were losing their spot next to the fence. It was now ten fifteen, and fans were arriving by the dozen, crowding in as the first fancy player's car pulled up and in—a Mercedes convertible.

Mr. Starr kept going, backward up the hill. "They're not going to help us and Thomas Trent isn't stopping for anybody."

"Are we going to get tickets?"

"No," Mr. Starr said. "Help me get this chair up the hill so we can get around this infernal fencing."

Ryder turned the chair and pushed it up the hill. They were approaching the police entrance when the fencing stopped and Mr. Starr said, "Now get this thing down over the curb."

"Mr. Starr, that's the street." Ryder looked up and down. Cars streamed past doing thirty miles an hour, at least.

"Do I have to run this thing off the curb myself and crash it?" Mr. Starr's voice had that edge again.

Ryder glanced at the police entrance. No one was watching them. He took hold and backed the chair off the curb. A car heading their way swerved without beeping its horn.

"Mr. Starr!"

"We're fine. They won't hit us. There's plenty of room for them to get by. They're just being difficult." Mr. Starr was speaking fast. "Go back down about halfway and we'll wait until we see Thomas Trent's Maserati. When we do, you run me down the hill and we set up right in front of the driveway.

He won't be able to go in and we can tell him that they promised us an autograph. You give him the ball, tell him you're his son, and say you have to talk to him after the game."

"It's just . . ." Ryder winced as another player went rushing past in a Range Rover. "I don't think this is the way to do it. This is so extreme."

"Yes, it certainly is," Mr. Starr said. "And so is your mother's condition, isn't it?"

Ryder stopped and clenched his teeth. This was all for his mom. He nodded his head, looking up the hill for a sign of the blue Maserati.

Suddenly, Mr. Starr mumbled, "Uh-oh."

Ryder turned.

"Well, well," Mr. Starr said. "Look who decided to show up."

Marching toward them was the security guard from the day before, the one with slicked-back hair and sunglasses, who'd promised to help.

"My boy," Mr. Starr said. "Our luck has just taken a turn."

## 47

"Hey, old-timer." The guard with the sunglasses smiled and his teeth flashed white surrounded by the dark beard and mustache. "Heard you started some trouble already. What're you doing out here in the street? You know you can't be here. You're gonna cause an accident."

"Old-timer? Why don't you just call me Crooked-man?"

"Hey, no need to get hot." The guard held his hands up in surrender and spoke in the pleasant tone of a friendly neighbor. "Why don't you two come with me? I can get you right inside where you won't get run down."

The guard waved his hands at an oncoming car and he motioned for them to go around. Ryder tightened his grip on the chair and began easing it down the slope toward the driveway with the security guard waving cars aside. The crowd of fans gaped with open mouths when they saw Ryder and Mr.

Starr on the inside of the fence with a security guard escorting them.

Mr. Starr snickered. "See what I mean, Ryder? Grease."

The guard led them right through the crowd and in through the player parking lot gates. Ryder looked over his shoulder, just praying for the blue Maserati to appear. It didn't, but the guard led them to a wide-open entrance leading into the stadium.

"This is where the players go in." The guard waved his arm in welcome. "Come right in."

"Well, we can wait out here," Ryder said.

"No, you guys just come with me. I've got the perfect spot for you to wait, and you won't be getting in the way when people are trying to park. That could get me into trouble."

"We don't want to get this fine young man into trouble, Ryder." Mr. Starr's eyes blazed with delight. "And if he's got a better place, why shouldn't we take it?"

Ryder shrugged and the guard punched the button on an elevator. It dinged and the doors opened.

"Right this way, gentlemen."

"The locker rooms are upstairs?"

"Actually, downstairs." The guard smiled big.

Ryder wheeled the chair inside. The doors closed, but the elevator heaved upward.

"I thought the locker room was down," Ryder said.

"Oh, this darn thing has a mind of its own sometimes." The guard hammered the back of his fist against the buttons to prove it and the B light went on.

They stopped at the floor above.

When the doors opened, two Atlanta City Police stood

173

with their arms crossed, waiting.

"Well?" The sound of Mr. Starr's voice didn't contain an ounce of respect or fear for the police. "Are you getting on? Are you going down, or what?"

One of the cops, a sergeant with three gold stripes on his short-sleeved black shirt, smiled at the security guard, then Ryder, and finally at Mr. Starr before he spoke.

"No," he said, "I'm not going down, and neither are you."

# 48

"This man promised to take us to meet Thomas Trent!" Mr. Starr's shriek made Ryder's hair stand up.

Ryder stood aside as the sergeant stepped in and took hold of the chair, wheeling Mr. Starr right off the elevator. Ryder followed.

"You can't stalk the players, sir." The security guard's friendly face had fallen flat. "Wheelchair or no wheelchair, you're being a menace."

The guard held the button that kept the doors open and he asked the sergeant, "You need me to sign anything else?"

"No. We got your statement and we got your partner's." The sergeant gave a short nod.

"Because they were at it again," the guard said. "Right out in the street, the two of them. I'm sure they were waiting for Thomas Trent."

"Of course we were waiting! You promised us an autograph! An introduction! Now, you do *this*?" Mr. Starr struggled in his chair, as if trying to break free, but the second cop restrained him.

"Easy, sir. Don't make this worse than it is. Look, you're embarrassing the kid." The sergeant surged ahead, rolling Mr. Starr down some back hallway.

Mr. Starr scowled at Ryder as though Ryder's silent horror somehow made him a traitor.

Ryder couldn't believe this was happening. He wanted to scream at them all. He was trying to save his mother's life, and Mr. Starr's approach wasn't getting it done. They should probably get out of there and make another plan. "Mr. Starr, maybe we—"

"I don't care! You people are liars! Where are you taking me?"

"You can't throw yourself in front of people's cars, and you can't wheel that thing around in a busy street. Where you go is up to you." The sergeant rolled Mr. Starr through a door the other cop had swung open.

Ryder looked around and realized they were in the Atlanta Police's office inside the stadium, the same one he'd seen the officers gathered around the entrance to on the outside. Sitting in chairs along one wall were two men, bruised and bleeding, who looked like they'd been in a fight. One wore a Braves T-shirt while the other had on the top of a torn Dodgers uniform. Each had his hands zip-tied together. Both looked miserable.

Mr. Starr was wheeled into a side room with a table and

two chairs bolted to the floor. The sergeant nodded at the seat on Mr. Starr's side of the table and Ryder took it. The other cop appeared with a clipboard and stood while the sergeant sat down and began to write down Mr. Starr's side of the story.

The sergeant seemed patient, which made Ryder feel even worse about the whole thing and especially the way Mr. Starr didn't let up being grouchy. He talked to the sergeant the way he talked to Doyle, barking and growling and insulting him at every turn with words like "meathead" and "donut fiend."

As the sergeant rose, Mr. Starr offered a parting shot. "I can't wait to see your face when they rip those stripes right off your sleeve. I'm going to come down on you so hard with the ACLU and the AAPD lawyers that they'll ban you and the next five generations of flatfoots in your family from working on a police force. You can't do this to me and you know it."

The sergeant clenched his teeth and turned around to glare right back at Mr. Starr. "I don't know who you think you are, sir. I'm sorry you're not well and I'm sorry you're in a wheel-chair, but it doesn't give you a free pass to break the law. Now, you want to talk about banning someone? Hear me on this, Mr. Starr. You're the one who's banned. You're banned from Turner Field. I'll pass your picture around to every security guard and cop at this stadium and if anyone so much as catches a glimpse of you, I'll have you two right back in here again, only next time, I'll load you both right up, chair and all, into the wagon and ship you downtown to the judge with the drunks and the fighters and you can tell him all about it. How do you like that, sir?"

Mr. Starr opened his mouth but nothing came out.

"Mr. Starr?" Ryder looked from his friend to the sergeant in panic. "He didn't mean it, Sergeant. He's just . . . grouchy, a little."

"No, a lot." The cop glared at Ryder now. "Son, it's over. You two are done here. Officer Brandy will see you back to your hotel, but I'm warning you . . . you two stay away from the Braves and Turner Field and especially Thomas Trent."

When they got back to the hotel, Officer Brandy saw them into the front entrance. Mr. Starr sat silent and glaring in his chair without meeting the curious eyes of the two women at the front desk. When Ryder pushed him around the corner into the hallway Mr. Starr said, "Stop."

Ryder stopped. "Are you okay?"

"Go see if the cop's still there," Mr. Starr commanded.

Ryder peeked back around the corner and saw a flash of the black uniform as the cop disappeared in the direction of the stadium. "He's leaving now."

"Good." Mr. Starr put his hand on the controller, turned the chair around, and began motoring toward the front entrance.

"Mr. Starr?" Ryder hurried to catch up.

The entrance doors slid open. The chair rattled and shook as Mr. Starr powered it over the threshold and out into the sunshine.

"Are you coming?" Mr. Starr asked.

"You want to eat?" Ryder eyed the Bullpen Rib House just across the parking lot.

"Not the Bullpen." Mr. Starr didn't try and hide his disgust. "You think we're going to give up that easy? We came all the way from New York City. You think that cop's really going to keep us out of that stadium? Ha!"

"But . . . how can we get in? I think we need a different plan."

"No way. Right through the front gates, that's how. He's bluffing. I know cops. I worked with them for twenty-seven years on the crime beat for the paper. They love to bluff. Bluff all the time. No one's going to notice us."

"Really?" Ryder's spirits soared at the thought of getting into the stadium. "If we did get in, maybe we could get Thomas Trent at the dugout when he comes out for warm-ups."

"Exactly. We'll scalp some tickets and go right in the front gate like everyone else. Now, get a hold of this chair and let's get going. It's faster when you push."

**49**

They got nosebleed tickets for twenty-five dollars each from a kid in a hooded Falcons sweatshirt who pretended Mr. Starr didn't exist.

Ryder felt guilty at the money he had to take out of Mr. Starr's wallet, but Mr. Starr told him it was free. Ryder pushed Mr. Starr right up to one of the main gates in front. Above them, the green steel frame of the stands towered over the red brick of the stadium. The smell of beer and popcorn and hot dogs filled the air. People flowed through the sunshine and into the stadium wearing Braves hats and shirts. The security guard stopped them and Ryder's heart skipped a beat. But the guard just waved a metal detecting wand around Ryder and then inspected Mr. Starr's wheelchair.

"You're gonna want to go in that gate with the wheelchair." The guard pointed to a big blue sign with a white stick figure in a wheelchair. "Enjoy the game."

Ryder pushed Mr. Starr toward the sign.

"See?" Mr. Starr sounded giddy, like an excited child. "I told you."

Ryder stopped at the wheelchair access gate. The other fans streamed through a turnstile. A female guard opened the gate and took their tickets. Then she looked at Mr. Starr and closed the gate quickly. "Hang on."

She walked over to another guard, this one a tall man with a big blond helmet of hair and a tan face. He looked at the tickets and then at Mr. Starr before taking out his iPhone. The guard looked at the iPhone and then at Mr. Starr again before walking over toward the gate with the other guard. When they got there, the tall man let himself through the gate before closing it.

"What's the problem?" Mr. Starr's voice had that shrill note suggesting hysteria.

"I'm sorry, sir," the guard said, "you can't come into the park."

## 50

"That is ridiculous!" Spit flew from Mr. Starr's mouth like misguided fireworks.

Ryder's heart sank. It was truly over now.

People all around were looking and the security guard's tan face reddened with shame for a brief moment. But the guard recovered his stern face and he shook his head.

"I'm sorry, sir." The guard's voice was soft but firm. "I'd lose my job. They sent a text around to everyone. Even if you got past me, they'd throw you out."

"I have a *ticket*!"

"I can call my supervisor. I'm sorry. That's all I can do."

"I thought you *were* a supervisor." Mr. Starr's voice lost its shrill edge; in fact, it had a begging quality to it that seemed to surprise the guard as much as Ryder. "Can't you help me?"

"I wish I could." The security man's eyes misted. "My

mother is in a wheelchair. I understand how you feel."

Mr. Starr just stared. Ryder thought of *Star Wars* and some mind-control trick, but the guard didn't budge.

"Then let the boy in." Mr. Starr's voice was hypnotic, neither weak nor obnoxious, just strong and certain.

The guard shook his head. "*I* can't do that."

"But someone else can?" Mr. Starr asked.

The guard looked around and lowered his voice even more. He kept his hand down at his waist and held out one of the tickets they'd given. "If he happened to go to another gate and you weren't there . . . well. I guess it might be hard to know he was even with you."

Mr. Starr looked at Ryder and nodded. "Take it," he whispered urgently, forcing the ticket into Ryder's hand.

Ryder looked around before pinching the ticket in his fingers and slipping it into his pants pocket.

Slowly, the guard let himself back inside the gate, eyeing Mr. Starr warily until it clanked shut.

Mr. Starr used the control to rotate the chair until he faced Ryder. "Get going."

"Alone?"

"Of course. You know what to do."

"I don't know . . . you'll be okay?" Ryder didn't feel comfortable at all going in alone.

"I'll meet you back at the hotel." Mr. Starr started to rumble off, cruising through the crowd, people parting for him right and left.

Ryder hurried to catch up. "That gate?"

Mr. Starr stopped his chair and flicked his eyes in the

direction Ryder pointed. "Yes. That gate will work fine. Don't worry. You can do this. Think of your mom."

Ryder choked on the idea of her lying there with those beeping machines. He swallowed and straightened his back. "Okay. I'll see you at the hotel."

"Don't forget me," Mr. Starr said, "if he decides to take you home for dinner or something."

Ryder flashed a smile back and he saw the smile in Mr. Starr's eyes if not his face. The idea lifted his spirits and he bounced on his toes as he waited in line at the next gate over. He began to worry about someone asking where his parent was, but they ran their wand over him and took his ticket without a word besides "enjoy the game." Ryder marched through the arch and up some stairs before he emerged inside the stadium. He blinked back the sun and shielded his eyes with a hand, locating the Braves' dugout.

Ryder worked his way through the stands and finally made it to the crowded area around the dugout where people pushed and wormed their way for position on the rail. Ryder felt some elbows, but he was determined to get close. When he finally broke through two older men and got to the rail, Justin Upton, the Braves' left fielder, was signing a couple gloves kids had brought before he held up his hands and disappeared into the dugout.

"Where's Thomas Trent?" Ryder cried out to no one in particular, the signed ball clutched tight in his hand.

Freddie Freeman, the Braves' first baseman, looked up as he hit the dugout steps, and chuckled. "Hey, kid, you won't get Trenty. He never comes out of the bull pen during warm-ups, but Tim Hudson will sometimes sign something."

Freeman disappeared and a string of other players filed into the dugout as the ushers began to shoo people away from the field toward their seats. Ryder clung to the rail with his free hand.

"Let's see your ticket, kid." A balding gray-haired usher put a thick hand on Ryder's shoulder.

Ryder held his breath, not knowing if he was going to be kicked out. He reached in his pocket and held out his ticket.

"This is for 502 out in left field, kid, in the upper deck."

"Is it near the bull pen?"

"Nowhere near it. You can't get autographs in the bull pen anyway, kid. Sorry. Get going, now." The usher didn't sound mean.

"Can you tell me how I can get Thomas Trent's autograph, mister?" Ryder held up his ball to show he was for real.

The usher's face practically lit up. "Sure, kid. That's easy."

"It is?" Ryder's blood raced. "How?"

# 51

"Autograph Day."

"Autograph Day?"

"They have it every spring." The usher was still beaming, but Ryder had a bad feeling.

"Like, it's coming up?" Ryder asked.

The usher scowled. "Well, no, it was three weeks ago, but there's always next year, kid."

"But I need it *now*," Ryder said.

"Well," the usher said, brightening again, "just wait after the game by the players' parking lot. Hold it through the fence and they sometimes will sign things. Depends on the day, how they played, that kind of thing, but . . ." He looked down at the ball Ryder was holding. "Hey, it looks like that thing already got signed."

The usher eyed him suspiciously now.

"Yeah. I . . . wanted to get it again. I mean, another one."
Ryder knew waiting after the game by the players' parking lot
wasn't an option.

"Okay, well, get to your seat, kid. This is the last time."

Ryder hurried away, and he did go to his seat. He stayed
and watched the game for a few innings. But Thomas Trent
was a faceless figure whose number Ryder could barely make
out in the bull pen. He watched Trent hit a double in the top
of the sixth, driving in the only run so far in the game and
lighting up the crowd. When the people around Ryder began
to sit back down, he decided to leave. As he left the ballpark
and crossed the street, he heard the roar of the crowd again and
knew something big must have happened, maybe a home run.
He tried to let the sound lift his spirits, but it didn't, and as he
walked through the front entrance to the hotel, tears blurred
the faces of the two women at the front desk.

Part of Ryder was afraid to face Mr. Starr, because after all
this, he had failed to get the job done. He felt certain he must
have missed something obvious, something Mr. Starr would
have figured out. It was unfair that Mr. Starr couldn't get in
when he had a ticket. It was unfair that his mother had been
struck by a car. It was unfair that his father left them alone over
twelve years ago and now he drove a Maserati.

Ryder opened the hotel room door with his key and saw
Mr. Starr sitting near the window. "I'm back," he said, his voice
glum.

"So?" Mr. Starr replied in anticipation.

Ryder sat on the edge of the bed and explained what had
happened.

187

"What will we do?" Ryder asked after silence settled in on the room.

"I don't know, Ryder. I need to think. Set that iPad up on the stand here at the desk. Maybe I'll play Candy Crush."

"You're not giving up?"

"I don't *give up*." Mr. Starr's voice was so bitter that Ryder stood up and looked out the window, where he could make out the green steel beams and brick of the stadium through the treetops. Mr. Starr sat, muttering to himself about police brutality and corporations sucking the life out of sports. Ryder opened the window, and through it heard the cheers spilling out of the stadium again so that he knew someone must have made another big play. He sighed and wondered what was next, even though he was afraid to ask.

It made him crazy to just sit there, not talking, and watching Mr. Starr struggle with the iPad.

"Can't I help?" Ryder asked.

"Nope." Mr. Starr's voice was a flat line, his limbs bent and jerky like a spider off of its web.

Ryder smelled the breeze and took in the sunshine. A truck rumbled past leaving behind a gray cloud of exhaust.

"Aha!" Mr. Starr exploded. "Aha! This is what we need. It's what we needed all along! I had such a feeling. You see, when things look their very worst, those who keep going are rewarded. I've seen it all the time."

"What reward?" Ryder turned and peered over Mr. Starr's shoulder. He had opened the *Atlanta Journal and Constitution* website.

"That's what happens when you *google*. You don't just google

'Braves.' You google 'meet the players' and google 'autographs' and regoogle 'Braves players' and google 'contest' and 'autographs' some more and then . . . then it *happens*. Just look!" Mr. Starr gave the machine a little shake with his crooked hand.

Ryder studied the screen. "It's a preview for the Dodgers game today. I don't get how that's a reward. Is there something about Thomas Trent in the article?"

"Not the article. The *ad*!" Mr. Starr shook it again. "On the banner there. Read it."

"The one for Baseball World?" Ryder knew about Baseball World. Back in New York, he'd heard his teammates talking about how their fathers took them to the one in Fort Lee, New Jersey, just over the George Washington Bridge.

"Yes." Mr. Starr was quickly losing patience. "*Read* it."

**52**

Ryder read aloud. "Batter Up, Braves Batboy *Contest*. It's tomorrow."

"Look at the *prize*."

"Be batboy for the Braves when they take on the St. Louis Cardinals in a doubleheader on Saturday, April 26th. Hey, that's the day after tomorrow." Ryder tried to read Mr. Starr's eyes. "So, I'm going to try and win this batting contest? Won't there be hundreds of kids, thousands?"

"So? Why can't you win it? I thought you were a good baseball player? I thought your mom always said you got that from your dad. He's batting .313 this season. If you're his son, you can win this."

"What do you mean *if*, Mr. Starr?" Ryder grew hot. "Why would you even say that?"

"Just what I said. We don't *know*."

"We came all this way."

"I know—"

"What will they even do at this contest?"

"Have you hit, what else? It's a batting cage place, so you'll bat in the cages."

Ryder's palms began to sweat. "I don't even have a bat."

"Well, we'll have to get you one."

"Maybe I should practice a little."

"We'll go there now and see what we can do."

"How can you even do that?"

"They have buses and trains. We'll get the bat at the mall and Baseball World is right on Peachtree so it can't be too far from a bus stop. Don't worry about that. It's our chance. I *know* it is."

## 53

While thousands of fans spent the afternoon at the Braves game, Ryder and Mr. Starr rode around on buses, got him a baseball bat and batting glove at Sports Authority in the mall, and found the closest stop to Baseball World. Signs for the contest were everywhere. It was for twelve-year-olds only and whoever could hit the biggest number of one hundred pitches from the machine would win. If there was a tie, they'd up the speed from seventy miles an hour to eighty-five and do a single-elimination contest. Kids could sign up online, or at the front desk. Ryder and Mr. Starr signed up at the desk. There was a thirty-nine-dollar entry fee. When they finished, they bought tokens for one hundred balls and found an empty cage in order to practice up for the contest.

Ryder swung his bat a few times to warm up, then he put a token in the red metal box next to the plate and the pitching machine whirred to life.

"You look like you know what you're doing." Mr. Starr spoke from where he sat, outside the cage.

"I haven't done it but it looks pretty obvious." The light went green on the box and Ryder stepped up to the plate. The pitching machine spit out a ball. Ryder could only blink as it clanked into the backstop behind him.

"You didn't swing." Mr. Starr let loose a squeak of a laugh. "*That* was pretty obvious."

"The balls are yellow." Ryder hit the pause button on the red box, crouched to pick up the ball from the concrete floor, and examined its dirty yellow surface. "And rubber."

"Well, they get a lot of abuse. You don't want them falling apart on you, right?"

"I wonder if it hits any different." Ryder was speaking to himself.

"A sphere is a sphere," Mr. Starr commented.

Ryder pressed Start, stepped up to the plate again, and this time hammered the pitch right back at the machine.

"That looked like a pro."

Ryder had to smile. He felt good and quickly got into a rhythm. Token after token he deposited into the machine and before they knew it, the red light went on, and he had no more tokens.

"How many do you think I hit out of those?" Ryder shouldered the bat and let himself out of the cage.

"You hit eighty-seven—that's if you include the nicks, the foul balls, and I gave you the benefit of the doubt on that first ball you let through."

Ryder nodded and began rolling Mr. Starr's chair back toward the clubhouse.

"Let's ask and see what won it last year. I gotta believe eighty-seven could take the cake," Mr. Starr said.

They asked. The man behind the cash register was busy and he glanced up at them, doing a double take before he forced his eyes away from Mr. Starr's frozen face. "Uh, well, there were three kids tied. They all hit ninety-nine, then we did a sudden death with the machine on big league speed. It only took four of those before there was only one guy left and he won."

"Wait," Ryder said, "*ninety*-nine?"

"Yeah. I get kids in here all the time. There's a knack to it, but I think it's mostly concentration. That's a lotta balls to hit, you know? Well, you do know because you just hit a hundred. How'd you do?"

"Uh, eighty-seven," Ryder said.

"Ouch," the man said.

Ryder looked at Mr. Starr. "Ouch is right."

## 54

After a quick dinner, Ryder and Mr. Starr took the bus back to the hotel just as the moon peeked up over the shoulder of the stadium as if to keep watch. Ryder pushed the wheelchair up the street into the face of a hot and dusty breeze. Two dark figures walked along the other side of the street, mumbling to each other and drinking something from a paper bag. Ryder hurried along. By the time they got to the air-conditioned room, Mr. Starr looked exhausted.

Ryder helped Mr. Starr into bed before washing up himself and collapsing into the bed by the window. He lay there in the dark for a long while and could hear the sound of the traffic on I-85 even over the steady hum of the air-conditioning unit. Ryder sighed louder than he intended.

"Can't sleep?" Mr. Starr's voice rose up from the darkness like a ghost.

"Ninety-nine, that's all I can think of. That and I wish there was another way. Couldn't we just try and go to his house?"

"Maybe if you hadn't pulled your stunt at Yankee Stadium," Mr. Starr snapped at Ryder. "We're on thin ice. If the police get a hold of us rolling around inside Country Club of the South, they won't just send us back to our hotel. They'll make some inquiries up in New York and they'll find out you're a fugitive."

"I'm not a fugitive." Ryder hated the sound of the word.

"Really? You're on paid leave?" Mr. Starr's voice hung in the darkness.

"Mr. Starr, Doyle says he'll get everything taken care of. This is all hard. Do you have to sound so crabby?"

The silence swelled all around him and Ryder began to regret his words.

"Tomorrow, I'll buy you a cupcake." Mr. Starr sounded sweet, but Ryder could tell he was forcing it.

Ryder burst out laughing and Mr. Starr brayed like a donkey. They laughed themselves out until it grew quiet again and Mr. Starr sighed.

"Go to sleep, Ryder. Tomorrow? You're going to hit a hundred."

"A hundred? How do you know?"

Mr. Starr sucked in some air, then yawned. "I just know. Our luck is bound to change. Now go to sleep."

# 55

They got up early and had breakfast in the dining room off the hotel lobby. Ryder wasn't too hungry, but managed a bit of Raisin Bran and a glass of orange juice. Mr. Starr seemed like he was getting ready to attend a birthday party and he practically bubbled with confidence.

"I'm nervous." Ryder made his confession as he wheeled Mr. Starr to the bus stop, the bat laid out over the handles of the wheelchair.

"Of course you are," Mr. Starr said cheerfully. "You're supposed to be. That's going to help you win this thing. It's all going to happen, Ryder."

"Mr. Starr?" Ryder stopped on the curb beneath the orange-and-blue-and-yellow MARTA sign.

"Yes?"

"I think I liked it better when you were crabby," Ryder

said. "It makes me less nervous."

"I don't care about you being nervous. I just told you that. You're supposed to be. Everything is riding on this."

"Jeez, Mr. Starr."

"Did you bring your baseball?" Mr. Starr asked.

"What? No." Panic filled Ryder.

"Well, why not?"

"Because . . . I'm not going to see Thomas Trent at this thing."

"No, but it's luck. It's an inspiration. Go get it."

"The bus will be here." Ryder's palms were sweating.

"Just go. You need that ball." Mr. Starr wasn't kidding.

"Mr. Starr?" Ryder hollered back. He was already jogging down the sidewalk back toward the hotel.

"I'm fine!" Mr. Starr shouted.

Ryder crossed the street, burst into the hotel, scrambled to their room, and dug the baseball out of his bag. He flew out of the room and sprinted back down the street, circling the stadium to where the bus would stop. The woman at the front desk had told them that the buses weren't as regular on a day where there wasn't any game, so he had no idea if he'd miss it or not. Ryder's side hurt and his throat burned. He saw the bus appear and round the corner where the stop was. He found a new gear and ran even faster, clutching the ball tight. When the bus came into view, he saw it had its wheelchair ramp out, but Mr. Starr was half on and half off of it, toggling his control back and forth.

As Ryder approached, he could hear the bus driver's shouts for Mr. Starr to stop fooling around. In the huge rectangular mirror up by the bus's front door Ryder could see the red, angry face of the driver looking back at Mr. Starr before he threw his hands in the air. Ryder huffed and gasped. He grabbed hold of the handles and pushed the chair up the ramp.

The driver shook his head and muttered and retracted the ramp before chugging on.

"You got it, right?" Mr. Starr asked.

Ryder couldn't speak, he only nodded and held up the ball.

"I hate when luck is necessary," Mr. Starr said calmly. "But it is in most things. Catch your breath and take a seat. I want you fresh for this contest."

Ryder did as he was instructed. They had to change buses at the Five Points station, but it wasn't more than an hour before they were rolling up the sidewalk along Peachtree Street to Baseball World. The parking lot was jammed and bright-colored balloons wobbled everywhere in the breeze, eager to tear away from the fencing, light posts, and clubhouse walls, none of them making it. Parents sandwiched their kids, baseball players all, most of whom wore their Little League uniforms as a point of pride. Ryder wished he had his team uniform, but he'd have to do his best in jeans and a T-shirt.

The worst thing, Ryder soon found out, was the wait. There were hundreds of kids. He got number 237 and found a place to sit. The steady sound of bats smacking balls in the cages worried away at Ryder's nerves. It was the sound of his undoing. Mr. Starr just sat, his eyes darting around at every player who crossed his field of vision, as if he were breaking them down, assessing their baseball skills.

Steadily, the numbers got called out over a loudspeaker.

During that time, Ryder stayed warm and loose by jumping up every few minutes, stretching, and lightly swinging the bat without too much power so as not to tire himself. It was a while, nearly two hours, but finally his turn came.

*"Number 237 report to cage sixteen. Number 237, you're on deck in cage number sixteen."*

"Let's go," Mr. Starr said. "This is it."

They watched the boy in front of Ryder struggle along and end up with just a sixty-two. Even though the kid was one of hundreds of contestants, it was somehow a relief to Ryder to see someone so much worse than him. A contest official sat in a folding chair with an iPad. His gut spilled down over his belt and he wore a Braves visor on his balding head. He sighed heavily and scratched his neck before dragging his fingers over the iPad and calling Ryder's name.

"Okay," Mr. Starr said, "let's go. Give me that ball to hold. Lock this thing up. I'm telling you, you're gonna get a clean hundred and win this thing outright."

Ryder forced a laugh. He opened the cage door and stepped inside. Heavy black netting sagged above him like a spider's web. His mouth was dry, his limbs felt shaky. He reached through the doorway and dumped his signed baseball into Mr. Starr's lap then wiggled his fingers into the glove. He took a couple practice swings, stepped up to the plate, and nodded at the contest official.

"Okay," the official said. "They come regular, so get reset quick after each pitch."

Ryder nodded again. "Got it."

The official pressed a button on the red metal box. The

light went green. The whirring machine clanked and clunked, then spit out a pitch.

Ryder thought about everything he had to do. He thought about Mr. Starr's confident cheer all morning and of the lucky baseball in Mr. Starr's lap.

He swung.

He missed.

# 56

The air in Ryder's lungs burst free, leaving him without any breath, oxygen-starved. He looked back at Mr. Starr through the cage.

"That's just one. You'll get the rest. You will."

Ryder couldn't believe Mr. Starr's certainty. It meant very little to him now. Mr. Starr had been wrong about Ryder batting a perfect hundred. All around him popping sounds of baseballs being smacked filled the air. He took a breath and shook his head.

The light blinked green and the next pitch came before he was ready. He swung and missed.

"Hey!" Mr. Starr's bark startled everyone around them, especially Ryder and the official, who adjusted his collar and gave Mr. Starr a squinty glare. "You can *do* this! You *have* to! Do you *hear* me?"

Ryder realized he was breathing again. He nodded his head and spoke to Mr. Starr in an urgent, hushed tone, but without taking his eyes off the machine this time. "All *right*."

The whirring machine clanked and clunked and spit out a burning pitch.

Ryder swung, hard.

POP.

Solid contact. The net jumped.

"One," the official announced, giving Ryder an awkward smile.

Ryder nodded and reset. The next pitch came.

POP.

"Two." The official didn't look up from his iPad, but he continued to count as Ryder continued to connect. Ryder swung the bat, over and over without even hearing the count.

"Thirty-three."

POP.

"Thirty-four."

Ryder's arms started to ache, but he didn't waver. One by one he went, swinging in an easy rhythm, thoughts of his mom's lovely smiling face filling his mind.

"Eighty-seven."

"You can do this!" Mr. Starr cried. "Keep going!"

He did. Swing after swing, he connected. Even when he barely nicked it, the official counted it. That's all he had to do was make contact. Those were the rules. The hazy sunshine swallowed him whole and the sounds from the other cages blurred into a dull and distant noise. All he heard now was the official's voice, counting out his hits.

"Ninety-six . . . ninety-seven . . . ninety-eight."

Ryder was in a full sweat. The machine hummed and went quiet. He looked at the official, whose eyes had brightened. "Wow. Super."

"Is that the most?" Ryder dropped his arms, the bat hanging loose in his hand.

The official shrugged. "We'll see. Last year it was—"

"Ninety-nine. I know, but I'm talking about today." Ryder bit the inside of his lip.

The official was intent on his iPad, touching the screen and studying it before looking up at Ryder with a grin. "Right now, you're in the lead."

Ryder felt the thrill of victory bubbling up from the center of his chest and making his head swim.

"There's a big leader board in the clubhouse," the official said. "You can watch from there if you want. It'll be a couple more hours is my bet."

"Mr. Starr, I'm in first." Ryder grabbed Mr. Starr's stiff and bony shoulder and looked into his smiling eyes.

"I just wish you hadn't missed those first two, but you did great, Ryder. You really did. Come on. Let's go keep an eye on things inside."

Ryder wheeled the chair down along the other cages, aware of the stares Mr. Starr drew from kids and parents alike and wanting to burst out and tell them all to look at him instead of Mr. Starr because *he* was in the *lead*.

Mr. Starr must have been thinking something similar because he suddenly started barking out to people. "Step aside. Champ's coming through. Step aside now. Champ's here. Step aside. . . ."

"Mr. Starr," Ryder whispered, "*please.*"

"What? They're all looking. Might as well let them know *who* they're looking at. I may be a freak show, but you are the champ."

"Not yet, Mr. Starr," Ryder said. "Isn't it bad luck to say you won before you really did?"

"We got our luck right here." Mr. Starr raised the signed baseball clutched in his claw. "Ninety-eight will do it. I feel it."

Ryder could only shake his head.

At the door to the clubhouse, a young father in jeans and a T-shirt carrying a little girl wearing a yellow dress came out. He stopped and shifted the little girl onto his hip so he could hold the door open for Mr. Starr. The man looked right at Mr. Starr without wincing or shifting his eyes and he said hi. Mr. Starr said nothing. The man smiled and said hello to Ryder as he pushed the chair through the doorway.

"Hi," Ryder said.

"How'd you do out there?" the man asked, cheerful as sunshine.

Ryder couldn't help beaming. "I'm in first, right now."

"Wow. You got that ninety-eight? We were just watching that on the board. You climbed right up."

"I climbed?" Ryder said.

"Yeah, every cage keeps the results pitch by pitch. After the first fifty it goes by percentage so you can see people climbing and falling. You got on the leader board and you just kept going. You passed everyone." The man tweaked his little girl's nose and kissed her forehead. "I told my stepson he's gonna have a tough time beating that. Anyway, good luck."

"Good luck to you, too." Ryder turned, feeling wonderful

now, and pushed Mr. Starr to a table where they could sit and watch the board as well as a big-screen TV that showed a game between the Red Sox and the Yankees.

"Why'd you wish him luck?" Mr. Starr sounded grouchy. "That wasn't smart."

"Why didn't you say hello? He was nice." Ryder didn't plan the question, it just came out.

Mr. Starr kept silent, his eyes flickering from the base-ball game on TV to the leader board without speaking. Ryder sighed and gave up before Mr. Starr finally spoke. "It surprised me, that's why. That's why I didn't say hello."

"Oh." Ryder didn't know how to respond. "You want me to get us some drinks?"

"Yes. Good idea. Don't forget a straw."

Ryder got up and, using money Mr. Starr gave him, bought some drinks. He tried to watch the baseball game, but his eyes spent more time on the leader board, watching certain names rise and fall and sometimes rise again. Over an hour went by and Ryder was beginning to feel pretty sure of himself when suddenly, a name popped onto the board ahead of him. A boy named RJ Leonardo appeared suddenly with fifty out of fifty—100 percent.

# 57

Ryder didn't bother with the game on TV anymore. His eyes were glued to the leader board, his throat suddenly scratchy and dry. He barely saw all the other people pointing at the screen, but they did and he was aware of it. A buzz of excitement filled the clubhouse as the families of the leaders and the hopefuls watched to see if the order of finalists would shift. Being batboy wasn't the only prize—the top ten finishers all got various lesser prizes. But to Ryder this was an all-or-nothing deal. If he didn't get to be the Braves' batboy, a signed bat or glove did him no good at all.

His life would be ruined unless he could get to Thomas Trent.

At RJ Leonardo's sixty-eighth hit, Ryder glanced over at Mr. Starr, whose eyes were also stuck to the board.

Mr. Starr looked over at him and held out the signed

baseball. "I told you, you shouldn't be wishing your luck away to total strangers. Here, you better hold on to this. You need it."

At seventy-two, RJ Leonardo had his first miss. The number fell to 99 percent, but RJ's name stayed on top.

Ryder took a deep breath. Mr. Starr clucked his tongue. "Just hold that ball tight."

Ryder held it so tight the laces seemed to be cutting into his skin. Every couple seconds, the number of hits kept climbing. It looked like RJ Leonardo wasn't going to miss another pitch.

Then, at pitch number eighty-four, RJ missed again, dropping him to 97 percent, and his name abruptly swapped out with Ryder's, which was back on top. Ryder gave the signed ball a shake.

"If he misses one more, we're good," Mr. Starr said.

"If he makes them, he'll get back to ninety-eight and it'll go to a tiebreaker," Ryder said.

"Which you'll win," Mr. Starr said confidently.

"I hope so," Ryder said.

"I know so," Mr. Starr replied.

The hits kept piling up and at ninety-eight the crowd in the clubhouse erupted, not with cheers, but with comments and observations about a tiebreaker between the two top batters. Ryder heard his name as people wondered aloud about who he was. Everyone seemed to already know RJ Leonardo. Apparently he was a batting ace from some top Atlanta travel team.

Ryder had such a strange feeling about RJ Leonardo, as if he'd heard the name before, or they somehow had some kind of a connection. So, when a boy in a green-and-gray uniform came through the door with people congratulating him, he knew it had to be RJ Leonardo and he wasn't surprised to see the nice man who'd held the door standing right beside him, holding the little girl's hand.

The boy was tall and strong and he had a friendly face like his stepfather as he grinned all around.

"What'd I tell you?" Mr. Starr grouched. "You never should have wished that guy luck. It was *his* kid."

"You said I'd win the tiebreaker anyway," Ryder reminded him.

"That was before I knew it was *him*. We're the ones with that signed baseball. That's our luck. You wished some of it away, and *directly* to him, no less." Mr. Starr's eyes were dead serious. "I can't be held responsible for what happens now. All bets are off."

# 58

Ryder tried to laugh away Mr. Starr's silly superstitions.

He didn't need luck. This was about skill. This was about nerve.

Ryder clenched his teeth and told himself he could do this . . . that he *would* do this. Over the past hour, while they watched the leader board flicker with names shuffling on and off the lower part of the list, Ryder's right forearm had cramped up and he had realized that he'd been clenching his fists as well as his teeth. Now, he massaged the muscles, hoping he hadn't put himself at a disadvantage in the tiebreaker with a sore arm.

Moments later, an official with an all-red baseball cap walked in and announced that the contest was officially complete.

"Are RJ Leonardo and Ryder Strong here?"

Ryder raised his hand and so did RJ Leonardo from his

table in the corner, where he sat with his little sister and dad.

"Congratulations to both of you," the official announced. "What we do now is a sudden-death tiebreaker with the pitches coming in at eighty-five miles an hour. It shouldn't take long. In years past, the most anyone's hit in a row has been seven. So . . . if you boys will make your way to cage number one, we'll get started and have our winner."

Everyone in the place got up. People pointed and whispered. Ryder took hold of the wheelchair and guided Mr. Starr out the front doors and down the concrete walk, following the official and knowing that RJ Leonardo wasn't far behind. When they got to the cage, the official was fiddling with the pitching machine, adjusting the speed to a major league–caliber pitch of eighty-five miles per hour.

Ryder handed the signed ball to Mr. Starr and removed his bat from the place where he'd wedged it into the side of Mr. Starr's chair. He wiggled his fingers into the batting glove.

"I think you should keep this in your back pocket." Mr. Starr held the ball up with his crooked fingers.

"That's not going to be comfortable, Mr. Starr. Don't you think it could affect my swing?"

"Yes, it could affect your swing," Mr. Starr snapped. "It could fill it to the brim with luck and make you win."

"But I didn't have it when I hit ninety-eight. Maybe it's more lucky for you to have it. We are in this together, right?"

Mr. Starr's mouth opened and closed like he was a fish swallowing water. "Yes, we are. Okay. I don't think it will hurt us any, but do not wish him luck. Are we straight on that at least?"

"Okay, Mr. Starr." Ryder's insides quivered. He'd never hit

a pitch this fast before. He had no idea if he could connect with even one.

"We'll flip a coin to see who goes first." The official held up a quarter. "Then we'll take turns, one hit at a time until someone misses. If the first batter misses, the second one has to get a hit, or we continue. Ready, boys?"

RJ's stepdad patted him on the back as he entered the cage. Ryder tried to slip past the man, but he gave Ryder's shoulder a squeeze and said good luck.

Ryder looked from RJ's stepdad to Mr. Starr's burning eyes and said, "Thank you."

That was it. He entered the cage, called heads on the flip, and lost.

"First or second?" the official asked RJ.

"Second." RJ offered Ryder a smile and a nod.

Ryder could barely breathe. He thought about his mom, lying in that hospital bed, and all those machines. He opened his mouth, but nothing came out.

"Okay, let's get this show on the road," the official said. "Batter up!"

Ryder took a few practice swings and stepped up to the plate. His mind spun with images of his mom and the man who had to be his dad. If he won this, he could bring them back together. Maybe not forever, but most importantly, he could save his mother's life.

The green light flashed. The machine whirred and clunked and the pitch came at him in a blur.

## 59

Ryder swung and nicked it.

"Did he hit that?" someone from the audience called out.

"Yes." The official held up a thumb. "Any contact counts. Those are the rules. RJ, you're up."

Ryder took a deep breath and let it out slow as he stepped back.

RJ bounced into place and gave the official a nod.

The official pressed Start, the machine clunked and spit, and RJ swung.

POP.

A solid hit and people clapped.

Ryder looked around. Mr. Starr sat looking through the mesh of the metal fence just outside the door. RJ's stepdad stood not too far away, but between and all around them was a crowd of people, young players and parents alike eager to see the tiebreaker between two sensational batters.

Ryder stepped up and connected with the ball. Mr. Starr barked and cheered and the audience clapped for him as well.

"Nice one." RJ Leonardo stepped up.

POP.

Applause.

Ryder's turn and just as the machine clunked, something stung in his eye. He blinked and swung, but missed.

The crowd groaned.

Mr. Starr held the ball against the fence. His mouth worked open and shut without words. Ryder stood back and took a deep breath. RJ had an easy stance as he slipped into place, as if nothing of any importance were on the line.

The machine whirred and clunked.

The ball screamed across the plate.

# 60

CRACK.

The net jumped, so did RJ Leonardo.

The crowd cheered.

The sound might as well have been Ryder's spirit breaking. He was destroyed. Tears sprang up into his eyes and a sob wrenched free from his gut. He looked back at Mr. Starr, who still held the ball against the fence and whose cheeks each bore the glittering tracks of tears. RJ Leonardo burst out of the cage, slapping high fives with his stepdad and little sister and the perfect strangers who clapped his back.

Ryder slipped out too and tugged Mr. Starr through the parting crowd without a word.

Mr. Starr made a choking noise. "I should have had you hold it."

"That wasn't it, Mr. Starr." Ryder tried hard to keep his voice from quavering.

"What was it, then?" Mr. Starr sounded so bitter. "Tell me?"

"I got something in my eye . . . I . . ."

"*That's* luck! Bad luck, a speck in the air gets in your eye at just the wrong moment." Mr. Starr laughed bitterly. "I knew better."

Ryder thought about the moment when he pulled away from his mother on the sidewalk, something as tiny as a speck. He had luck all right, and all of it was bad.

Now that they were away from the crowd, Ryder felt alone and exhausted. He wheeled Mr. Starr into the parking lot, headed for the bus stop just down the road. They were halfway across the lot when someone shouted his name.

"Hey! Ryder Strong!"

Ryder turned.

"Who's that?" Mr. Starr struggled in his seat, unable to turn.

"It's . . . it's RJ Leonardo and his stepdad."

"Wait up!" the stepdad called as they hurried toward Ryder and Mr. Starr, weaving through the parked cars.

The little girl bounced up and down on the stepdad's shoulders. Her blond hair glinted in the sunshine and her giggling filled the air.

"Let's just go," Mr. Starr grouched. "What could he possibly have to say to you?"

Ryder didn't move. It wouldn't be polite, and his mother had taught him better.

RJ and his stepdad came to a stop in front of them.

"Hey, name's Rick Bernard, RJ's stepdad," the stepdad said. "That was some hitting. You were great."

"RJ was better. Congratulations. I . . . we just . . . had to get going."

"Oh, don't worry about that." Rick Bernard waved a hand through the air. "Look, I saw how upset you are and we don't need that gift certificate. You're welcome to it. You deserve it. I mean, really, it *was* a tie. Right, RJ?"

RJ grinned and nodded and held out a Sports Authority gift certificate for five hundred dollars. Ryder looked at Mr. Starr.

"You think this boy is crying over money?" Mr. Starr sounded mean. "You think he's some spoiled brat who cares about a new pair of shoes?"

"Mr. Starr, please don't." Ryder couldn't help the scolding sound in his voice.

"Please." Mr. Bernard never stopped smiling. "We didn't mean anything bad. We're just happy to—"

"Charity? Since you're so rich?" Mr. Starr seemed madder still at the sight of Mr. Bernard's smiling face.

"I'm sorry." Mr. Bernard lowered his voice and Ryder felt like the man must be some kind of an angel not to get mad right back. "Is there anything we can do? I just sensed something bigger is going on here . . . just from Ryder's face. He didn't look like he lost a contest. He looked like . . . well, like someone died or something."

Ryder felt fresh tears in his eyes. "I just . . . we need to go. Thanks anyway." Ryder turned to leave.

"I'm sorry. I'm right, aren't I? Something is very wrong. Come on, how can we help you?"

"You really want to help?" Mr. Starr raised his voice.

"Yes," Mr. Bernard said. "We really do."

"Let Ryder be the batboy for the Braves. That'd help."

Ryder could tell by the look on RJ's face that it was the last thing he expected . . . and the last thing he wanted to do.

Mr. Bernard's smiling face fell, and his eyes hardened.

# 61

"Well, that's kind of why RJ did this whole thing." Mr. Bernard struggled to regain his smile.

"Of course," Mr. Starr said.

"I understand why you're bitter, sir," Mr. Bernard said.

"You understand nothing." Mr. Starr's eyes burned.

"We have box seats right behind home plate," Mr. Bernard said. "You could be our guests if you'd like."

"Ryder *needs* to be the batboy," Mr. Starr said. "That's the problem with people like you. You want to go through life, regifting the ugly sweaters or neckties someone gives you at Christmas and expecting people to think you're a saint. You're not a saint. You're just like everyone else, so you can stop smiling and holding the door for people, thank you."

Mr. Bernard huffed. He glanced at his son and shook his head. "I can't believe this."

"Ryder's mother is *dying*. It's a long and incredible story, but if he's the batboy, it could save her life," Mr. Starr said.

Mr. Bernard laughed in disbelief. "I don't think so," he mumbled.

"That's right. It's crazy," Mr. Starr said, "but it's true. I won't bore you with the details. That way when you say your prayers tonight, you can ask God to watch over the crazy guy in the wheelchair with that kid who you *tried* to help by giving a five-hundred-dollar gift certificate. That'll be a good prayer for you. Come on, Ryder, get me out of here."

Ryder took hold of the chair. His face burned with embarrassment and he couldn't look either RJ or his stepdad in the eye as he started to push away.

"Wait." Mr. Bernard put a hand on Ryder's shoulder and gently turned him around. "Is this really true?"

Tears streamed down Ryder's face and he bit hard into his lower lip to keep quiet as he looked at Mr. Bernard and nodded his head. "I think Thomas Trent is related to me. My mom needs an operation, like, right now. I think if I can talk to him, he'll help. That's why being batboy is so important. It's a way for me to get close to him."

Mr. Bernard read Ryder's face, and his own face softened, just like his voice. "Well, then. You can tell your friend that he's very wrong about me *and* my son."

"Dad? What are—" RJ cried.

Mr. Bernard turned to RJ. "I have an idea," he said, taking the envelope from RJ's hand.

"What is it?" Ryder asked.

"It's the paperwork for being batboy," RJ's dad said. "You

got to fill it out and bring it with you. There's a PR guy you're supposed to call in the morning, Ethan Kupec. The instructions are here on where you have to go and everything. Now, it's a doubleheader, so I'm going to propose that we meet at the PR offices after the first game. This way, RJ can be the batboy for the night game. Would that work?"

Ryder grinned so hard he couldn't speak, but only nod his head.

"All right," Mr. Bernard said. "I'll take care of all the details with the Baseball World people and the team so they'll be expecting you tomorrow instead of RJ. Good luck, Ryder. I hope this helps your mom."

"Me too," RJ said. "See you after the first game."

Ryder took the envelope and spoke in a whisper. "Thank you so much."

Mr. Bernard mussed his stepson's hair and grinned at Ryder and they turned and walked back across the lot, accepting congratulations from random people headed for their cars.

Mr. Starr sighed. "I told you it was meant to be."

"Mr. Starr . . . you didn't say thank you."

"Don't worry." Mr. Starr's voice was quiet and calm. "*He* knows."

"What should we do?" Ryder asked.

"Do?" Mr. Starr harrumphed. "Get me back to the hotel. We'll get some barbeque at the Bull Pen and plan our attack. Then we'll get some sleep so you're ready for tomorrow. You're gonna be the Braves' batboy, and you're gonna meet your father."

## 62

When Ryder woke the next morning, sunlight was already punching through the cracks in the curtains. He sprang up and looked over at Mr. Starr, who lay wide-eyed on the other bed.

"Figured I'd let you get caught up on your sleep, but we should get some breakfast."

Ryder helped Mr. Starr out of bed and into his chair.

"Hopefully we can wrap this up today," Mr. Starr said with a grunt as he sat down in his wheelchair.

"Do you think?" Ryder's frame already trembled at the thought of meeting his father and—if things went as planned—saving his mother.

"When you show him that ball and he realizes you're his son," Mr. Starr said, "I think he'll be happy to help. He'll want to keep this thing quiet, they always do, and we'll be on our way back to New York with a big check . . . or the promise of one, anyway."

Ryder frowned. "Why do they always want to keep it quiet?"

"I told you before. He's got his life, you've got yours. He's probably going to want to keep it that way."

"But . . . you never had kids, Mr. Starr. Maybe he'll want to stay in touch."

"Maybe." Mr. Starr's eyes looked dead, but then they brightened. "Let's get you cleaned up and dressed and call that Braves PR person, what's his name?"

"Ethan Kupec."

"Right. Shower, breakfast, then Ethan Kupec to confirm where to go."

Ryder got cleaned up. He put on fresh jeans and a clean blue T-shirt and wheeled Mr. Starr to breakfast. Ryder helped Mr. Starr eat his eggs, then scarfed down a plate of eggs and bacon. They returned to the room so Mr. Starr could make the call.

"Hello? Ethan Kupec?" Mr. Starr flicked a crooked hand at Ryder, telling him to raise the phone up higher. "Rick Bernard got in touch with you yesterday. Ryder Strong and RJ Leonardo won the Baseball World batboy contest, and they are going to share the opportunity. I wanted to follow up and make sure he's all set to be batboy for the first game, and RJ will come in for the second game. It says here he just goes to the media gate at noon."

Mr. Starr listened and Ryder could hear the buzz of the man's voice.

"Yes, he's got all the release paperwork signed by his parents,"

Mr. Starr said. "You'll see him at noon right there. Thank you. His name is Ryder, Ryder Strong . . .

"Yes, it is an unusual name, and he's an unusual young man, as you'll see. He's very excited. Yes. Thank you."

Ryder took the phone away and hung it up on the table between the beds. "I don't have anything signed."

"I can sign that if you put the pen in my hand. Adults don't read signatures. And you'll be going into the park yourself. I can't. Not after two days ago."

Ryder nodded. He hadn't ever considered that he'd have to do this thing all by himself, but of course he would. Mr. Starr would stand out like a flashing light and they'd be apt to get bounced right out again, contest or no contest.

"Oh, don't look like that," Mr. Starr said. "You can handle this. You'll be fine."

"For some reason me and baseball stadiums don't seem to mix." Ryder thought of being caught in Yankee Stadium. It seemed so long ago that he had to really think about it to make it seem real.

"All that changes in about an hour, right?"

"Yes," Ryder said. "You're right. Maybe we should call Doyle? I'd like to talk to him, not email."

"You want to check on your mom?" Mr. Starr backed his chair up and buzzed over toward the window that looked out over the city of Atlanta with its golden-domed capitol building. "I think that's a good idea. Get yourself focused on what this is all about. Go ahead."

Ryder dialed Doyle, who answered on the first ring.

"Hey, partner. Your ears must've been ringing." Doyle was

out of breath. "Did you talk to your dad?"

"Not yet," Ryder said.

"Well," Doyle said, "I just got some great news."

"About my mom?" Ryder's heart soared.

# 63

"Well," Doyle said, still excited, "it's kind of about her. I mean, there's been no change, but it's about FDNY. I got it, buddy! I got the logo! I can start fund-raising with it. Isn't that awesome?"

"Yeah." Ryder was a bit confused. "I mean, does this mean I don't have to ask my dad for the money?"

"Well, no." Doyle cleared his throat. "I think you still should. It's just that, I don't know . . . I can help, you know."

"Oh. Sure." Part of Ryder was disappointed, but another part was relieved because he *wanted* to meet his father. He wanted Thomas Trent to know he was *alive*. "Well, that's great, Doyle. I appreciate that."

"Happy to help. You know that." Doyle's smile was easy to imagine through the phone. "So, you didn't meet him? When I read your email about it being a big day and I didn't hear from you, I thought maybe . . ."

"No, but hopefully later. Um, how's my mom? Is she talking?" Ryder asked.

"She's still pretty foggy because of all of the pain medication, buddy, but she looks good. Strong, like you. Positive thoughts, remember?"

"Honestly, I don't feel so strong." Ryder flicked his eyes at Mr. Starr, but of course Mr. Starr didn't move or give any indication that he'd even heard.

"Well, you are. Look at you, down in Atlanta and you think you're going to meet your dad?"

Ryder looked at the clock and his heart began galloping again. "In about a half hour, maybe."

"You don't know for sure?"

"They had this batting contest at a place called Baseball World," Ryder explained. "The winner got to be an honorary batboy for the Braves today. I guess it's a big deal because batboys are supposed to be fourteen, but they made an exception for this contest so there were tons of kids."

"And you won? That a boy! See what positive thinking does?"

"That's the funny thing. I didn't win. This kid, RJ Leonardo was his name. *He* won, beat me in a playoff, but there's a doubleheader game today, so we're splitting the prize."

"That's an awesome story, buddy." Doyle chuckled. "Seems like luck is on your side."

Ryder picked the signed baseball up off the table between the beds. "Yeah, seems like it."

Mr. Starr's wheelchair began to hum as he backed away from the window. "Do you really have to give him all the details? I thought you didn't have a lot of minutes on that thing."

Ryder nodded. "Okay, Doyle. I gotta go."

"I heard that old grump grouching at you," Doyle said. "Tell him I said to put a sock in it."

Ryder smiled. "Okay, I'll tell him. Gotta go. Kiss my mom for me. Bye."

Ryder hung up and could tell by the look of Mr. Starr's eyes that he was disgusted.

Mr. Starr gave a snort. "Do you realize you just told that buffoon to kiss your mother?"

"I said, you know, from me."

Mr. Starr huffed. "All right. Let's get you going. You ready?"

"I'll be early," Ryder said.

"Early bird gets the worm. Don't they teach you kids anything anymore? It'll take you time to get there, and if the media gate is half as incompetent as the security crew, they'll need extra time to figure out who and what you are."

"I've got this pass, though, and Mr. Kupec's waiting for me." Ryder took the special media pass from the envelope RJ had given him. "You've got to sign this, though."

Ryder set the ball down. He helped Mr. Starr fit a pen into his right hand and placed the liability waiver on the desk where he scrawled out a squiggle that Ryder supposed could pass as a signature.

"You going to wait right here?" Ryder asked.

"Better that they don't see me, you know that."

Ryder took a deep breath and looked around. There was nothing more to be done. He turned and put his hand on the doorknob.

"Ryder!" Mr. Starr's bark startled him.

"What?"

Mr. Starr snorted at him. "The ball. You forgot the lucky ball."

"Oh." Ryder felt his face heat up. "Thanks."

"Can you imagine going in there without it? 'Hi, I'm Ryder, remember Ruby?' Come on. Be sharp." Mr. Starr glared. "He needs to *see* that ball."

Ryder retrieved the ball and left the hotel room in a daze. He stumbled through the lobby and out the automatic doors into the sunlight. The smells of game day hit him—hot dogs, beer, and bus exhaust—turning his stomach. He crossed the nearly empty street and headed down through the gallery of whispering trees. Fans were few and far between and only a few police officers talked over paper cups of coffee in the shade.

Ryder saw the media gate and walked right up to the black metal bars. It was locked. He turned to go when he saw a man with a laptop computer case wearing shorts and a flouncy polo shirt swing open a small door cut into the bars in the far corner of the big gate. Ryder started toward him and the man stopped and held the door for him.

Ryder lifted his media pass in the air and the man nodded as he let him through. "*Sports Illustrated for Kids* or something?"

"Batboy for the day," Ryder said. "I won a contest."

"Another contest. I wish we could hit as well as we run contests," the man said. "If we did, we'd sweep the pennant this year. Come on. You probably need to see Ethan Kupec, right?"

"Yes," Ryder said.

"You can follow me." The man stopped and looked at Ryder's hand. "Wait. What's that?"

"Just . . ." Ryder gripped the ball tight. "A baseball."

"To get signed?" the man asked.

"Yes." Ryder's voice was a whisper.

The man shook his head, scowling. "No way. They'll never let you in with that thing. You're a batboy, not some autograph hound. The rules are very strict. Here, you can give it to me and I'll hang on to it for you."

The man held out his hand and Ryder swallowed hard.

## 64

The man suddenly burst out laughing. "Ha! Got you. Come on, kid. You're fine."

The man mussed Ryder's hair and tugged him by the arm through the gate.

"Just kidding." The man grinned at him. "You should've seen your face."

Ryder followed the man into the stadium. They passed two guards who glanced at their passes and then continued across a small courtyard and through a glass door with the Braves logo plastered across it. The air-conditioning hit Ryder hard, but his armpits continued to sweat, even harder. They walked past a set of elevators and through another door where desks sat in clusters throughout a big room. In one corner was an office partitioned off by glass. Its windows looked out onto the playing field. Behind the desk sat a thin man of about thirty years old with spiky blond hair and a serious face.

"Hey, Ethan, got someone for you," the writer said, pushing the office door open and letting Ryder in before he disappeared.

"Ah, you're early," Ethan Kupec said, rising from his desk and extending a hand.

Ryder shook the hand and then gave the PR man his paperwork.

He glanced at it and put it on his desk. "No adult supervision for you, huh?"

"I got dropped off," Ryder said. "By my friend's dad."

His face grew a look of concern. "What about your parents?"

Ryder shrugged. "My mom's in the hospital. It's just me and her."

"Well, this is a nice thing to be doing, right? And you must have some super friends to give you the chance to be batboy for a day. Kids would kill for this." He pointed at the computer on his desk. "We get over a thousand applications every season, and only four positions. They get filled by people on the inside. That's between us, not that it's national news. The contest—I thought, anyway—was a nice way to give just anyone a chance, and here you are."

"Here I am." Ryder shifted on his feet.

"Well, let's go get you a uniform."

"Uniform?"

"Sure, batboys wear uniforms just like the players. That's half the fun, right? You get to keep it. Did they tell you that?"

"Can I get to meet some of them?" Ryder clutched his baseball, keeping it tight to the side of his leg so Kupec wouldn't

232

notice. "The players, I mean?"

He tilted his head and looked sideways at Ryder. "Meet them? You'll be working with them, handing them their bats, shagging Gatorades, whatever they want. You're *part* of the team today."

"And they . . . they don't mind talking?"

"Well, they're not gonna give you their life histories, but yeah, you can talk to them. I wouldn't get too chatty, but you don't strike me as the type. Are you?"

"What?"

"Chatty?"

Ryder shook his head no, but then wondered what the fallout would be if Kupec knew he was going to spring a huge question on their top relief pitcher. He imagined the PR man wouldn't be too happy. It made Ryder's mouth dry and he couldn't even swallow.

"You okay? Don't get nervous. These guys are just people like you and me. Come on. The best way to get over this is to just meet them." Kupec walked past him and swung open the door, looking back. "Come on."

"Where are we going?"

He laughed. "To the locker room."

Ryder followed, numb to the world around him. They went back the way he'd come and went down the elevators. There were security guards everywhere now. Ryder tried to keep his face angled at the floor in case anyone remembered the texted photo from two days ago. When they stepped off the elevator and walked down a long hall, the guard outside the locker room doors put up a hand, stopping Ryder. "Hey, kid."

Kupec stopped with his hand on the door and turned around. "What's the matter, Glen?"

Ryder thought he'd die.

"His shoe's untied." The guard smiled.

Ryder let out his breath and forced a chuckle as he bent down to tie his sneaker, which was awkward since he was holding the baseball and trying to keep it from sight at the same time he tied up. "Yes. Thanks."

When he had it tight, he gave Kupec a nod. The PR man smiled and swung open the door to the locker room. It smelled like leather and aftershave and new carpet. Sitting at his locker directly across from the door, lacing up his own shoes, was Thomas Trent. He tied off his left cleat, then looked up at Ryder and grinned.

# 65

Ryder went completely numb.

He had planned on waiting for just the right moment. He knew he should, a time when he could quietly slip alongside Thomas Trent and whisper his message. Even as his feet took him across the fresh carpet and he heard Ethan Kupec's question, asking him what he was doing, he also heard a voice inside his head, hollering for him to *wait*!

He couldn't wait, though. Halfway across the floor, he held out the baseball for Thomas Trent to see. Thomas Trent gave a pleasant look to Kupec and smiled awkwardly at Ryder. "Hey, little buddy. Need a signature on that thing?"

In a voice that sounded like it came from a can, Ryder heard Kupec apologetically explain who Ryder was, a batting contest winner, batboy for a day, obviously starstruck by his first real-life Braves player. Ryder was remotely aware of other players sitting around, but he couldn't say whether they were smiling or frowning and he didn't care. He was drowning in the pale green eyes of the man he just knew was his father. He wanted to laugh and he wanted to cry.

Thomas Trent took the ball from him and chuckled and looked at Kupec. "You got a Sharpie for me?"

Ethan Kupec did have a Sharpie and before Ryder could produce his own pen the PR man handed it to the pitcher as he apologized again on Ryder's behalf. He chided Ryder, saying that he really wasn't supposed to be getting autographs. He was a batboy and there to work.

"That's not a big deal." Thomas Trent took the cap off the Sharpie and turned the ball over in his hand. "Where do you want me to sign it, buddy? Someone already got the middle of this one. It's an oldie, too, huh?"

Thomas Trent turned the side with his old signature away from him without even looking and pointed to another open spot on the bottom of the yellowing ball. "By the MLB logo? That good?"

Ryder just stared. Thomas Trent glanced up at Kupec and raised his eyebrows. "Okay, I'll just sign it here for you."

He signed the ball in the open space below the MLB logo and handed it back to Ryder. Ryder didn't know how he knew, but he knew he wasn't going to see Thomas Trent again. He suspected that after this uncomfortable incident, Kupec was going to keep him under wraps for the rest of the day. The fog wouldn't clear from his head and he had no idea what to say or do, only that the situation was getting more uncomfortable by the second.

"Okay, well, thank you so much, Thomas." Kupec put a firm grip on Ryder's shoulder and turned him around to go.

It was everything or nothing now. Ryder knew that. He'd come so far, but he was painfully aware that everything in these past few days had gone against him, everything. It was like the Midas touch in reverse. Instead of everything he touched turning to gold, it turned to garbage. Still, he had to do something.

He had to try.

## 66

He started to go along with the PR man, but only for two steps, then he ducked and spun and darted at Thomas Trent, brandishing the ball like a weapon.

"You signed it twice!" His shout turned every head in the locker room. "Look! You signed it already! For Ruby! In Auburn! You were with the Doubledays! You called her your gem! I'm her *son with you*! Mr. Trent, you've got to help us, *please*! She's *dying*!"

Time stopped.

Thomas Trent's mouth had fallen open and Ryder was struck by the stains on his teeth and the silver fillings in the back molars. His eyes swam with confusion and maybe something else, maybe fear. The Atlanta Braves players stood or sat frozen, as if under the spell of an evil witch. Ethan Kupec sucked in a quick breath and held it, frozen as well.

Then everything happened at once. Tears sprang into Ryder's eyes. Hands were on him, pulling him, lifting him off his feet, and the players roared with chatter and some broken laughter about the crazy kid stalking Thomas Trent. Ryder tried to resist without fighting. He let his legs go limp and dragged his feet and watched Thomas Trent, praying for a miracle, thinking positive thoughts the way Doyle told him he should.

Thomas Trent looked down at the ball in his hand. He turned it to the old autograph, the one he'd signed for Ruby over twelve years ago, and his face twisted in disbelief. He looked up at Ryder, but his eyes were full of fear. Everything Mr. Starr said about Thomas Trent wanting to protect his own life flooded Ryder's mind.

"*Please!*" Ryder's shriek cut through the locker room noise and he sobbed. "You've got to help her, Mr. Trent. *You've got to! I'm your son!*"

Ryder heard the doors behind him banging open. More hands were on him, strong hands with iron grips, and he was lifted into the air and carried out into the hallway. In the chaos of the locker room, Ryder saw Thomas Trent in the middle of it all. Their eyes locked on each other's until the door slammed shut and they marched him up the long hallway like a criminal, away from the field, away from the clubhouse, away from Thomas Trent.

## 67

On the sidewalk outside the stadium, Ryder felt like a deflated beach raft. He slumped along, with Ethan Kupec tugging him by the arm. The furious PR director delivered Ryder personally back to the hotel room. Ryder couldn't even talk, and Mr. Starr seemed to know what had happened, because instead of asking questions, he turned the TV on to the Braves game.

The PR director left, and Ryder and Mr. Starr sat in silence, watching the game. In the bottom of the third, tears began streaming down Ryder's cheeks. "He just stood there, Mr. Starr. He didn't say anything and they . . . they just took me away."

Mr. Starr cleared his throat. "I'm putting a curse on that man."

"A curse?"

"Yes."

"Mr. Starr?"

"Just let's see if there's any justice left in the universe. Let's watch this game and see what happens and let me think."

The whole thing sounded crazy to Ryder, but he nodded his head and sat back against the headboard of his bed.

The Braves replaced Mike Minor in the top of the eighth with a two-run lead and Thomas Trent jogged out to the mound with the crowd cheering so loud Ryder could hear it outside the hotel window. But Trent couldn't close it. He gave up four runs before they pulled him for Luis Avilan. The Braves ultimately lost 6–7.

"Yes!" Mr. Starr trembled in his chair, shouting at the TV. "That's what a curse does to you!"

In a quieter voice, he said to Ryder, "You can turn that off now."

Ryder flicked the remote and their room, like the stadium across the street, was now totally silent. "What now?"

"Now?" Mr. Starr said. "We wait."

"Mr. Starr . . ."

"He knows he's been cursed."

"Mr. Starr." Ryder didn't want to depend on hocus-pocus, he wanted to *do* something. "Maybe we should try to get into where he lives. Maybe *I* should. I mean, I know we can't take a bus and we can't walk through the front gates, but maybe I can sneak in . . . climb the wall or something?"

Mr. Starr toggled his control to spin the chair around toward Ryder's bed. "To what end?"

"To . . . to talk to him. Without everyone all around."

"You planted the seed," Mr. Starr said. "Now we have to let it grow. It all depends on whether or not Thomas Trent has a conscience. If he does, we'll hear from him. If not . . . well, let's be optimistic. He can't like what happened to him on the mound today. That's got to get him thinking."

"About a curse?"

"Yes, a curse," Mr. Starr said. "Whether he knows it came from me or not, it's karma. He knows the universe is out of balance because of *him*. He *feels* it. Besides, athletes are extremely superstitious."

Ryder clenched his teeth.

"Come on, let's splurge and watch that new James Bond movie. I'm buying." Mr. Starr spun his chair back toward the TV.

It was hard for Ryder to concentrate, but when James Bond flew a helicopter through the streets of New York City, it distracted him enough to let him lose track of time. As the credits rolled, there was a knock at the door.

Ryder's insides squirmed. He stared at Mr. Starr.

"Open it." Mr. Starr sounded like he knew something Ryder didn't.

Ryder crossed the room and heard Mr. Starr's chair buzz as it spun toward the door.

He fumbled with the handle and pulled it wide.

Thomas Trent stood there, scowling at Ryder as he held out the ball he'd signed thirteen years ago and again today.

## 68

Ryder looked at the ball.

Thomas Trent gave it a little shake and let it lie in his open palm. "Here. It's yours. Take it."

Mr. Starr remained silent. Ryder took the ball and looked up at the Braves' pitcher.

"Can I come in?" Trent's dark hair was flat and still wet from a shower. He wore a brown suede blazer over an open-collar shirt, with matching shoes. On his wrist was a watch so big it reminded Ryder of a gold plumbing fixture from the Pierre Hotel.

"Please do that." Mr. Starr raised his voice from within. "And don't let me frighten you. I was once an ordinary man and like to think of myself in those terms. The look of horror on people's faces makes that difficult at times."

They went into the hotel room and Ryder admired Thomas

Trent's attempt to control his facial expression when confronted with Mr. Starr's twisted shape.

"I'm Stephen Starr. You've already met your son, Ryder." Mr. Starr kept going, even though Thomas Trent winced at the word "son." "I'd shake hands but it's difficult for me."

"That's okay," Trent said. "I feel bad for Ryder. I know the whole thing in the clubhouse today was . . . it was pretty uncomfortable."

"Why? Because they dragged a twelve-year-old boy out of the stadium like a terrorist? Kids are too soft these days, don't you think?" Mr. Starr's dead stare seemed to unsettle Thomas Trent.

Trent shook his head and looked from Mr. Starr to Ryder. "I'm not your father, Ryder. I don't know who you are or how you got here or anything. If Ruby Cantorelli is your mom, then I certainly knew her, but if I was your *father*, well, that's something the Ruby I knew wouldn't have kept a secret like that. I just can't believe she'd ever say I was your father."

Ryder's eyes filled with tears. The bottom fell out of his world.

Thomas Trent stared at him for a moment, then in a quiet voice said, "She didn't say I was your father, did she?"

Mr. Starr gurgled, then spoke. "She didn't have to say it. Look at him. Same eyes. Same hair."

Thomas Trent turned to Mr. Starr. "Look, no disrespect, but there are millions of people with green eyes and dark hair."

"Dark *curly* hair." Mr. Starr's head trembled.

Thomas Trent ignored him and spoke quietly to Ryder. "I'm sorry. I'm sure this is all real tough, kid. Maybe I can get

244

together some signed stuff to help out with a fund-raiser for your mom."

Ryder folded his arms and tried not to sob. Tears fell straight from his face to tap the carpet. He couldn't even get the number out of his mouth, two hundred thousand. He doubted whether there were enough bats, balls, uniforms, and caps in all of Turner Field that could be signed and sold off for that much.

"So, you do feel for this boy?" Mr. Starr sounded annoyed. "You're not just some callous self-infatuated egomaniacal sports star?"

Thomas Trent scowled at Mr. Starr. "No. I'm not."

"Wonderful." Mr. Starr sounded truly pleased. "Then I know you won't mind taking a paternity test to make sure you're really *not* Ryder's father."

"Listen, I'm not going to get involved in some kind of a scam thing." Thomas Trent raised his voice at Mr. Starr. "They warned me not to even come over here, but I wanted the kid to have his ball and I wanted to set him straight."

"It's not involved and this is not a scam!" Mr. Starr shouted Thomas Trent into silence before taking a breath to calm himself and speaking normally. "You can get one in a drugstore. You can rush the order and it takes a day. Swab your cheek. It's easy. It's simple and one hundred percent accurate."

Trent took a breath and glanced at Ryder. "I can't just do something like that. I'm not—"

"You afraid of the truth?" Mr. Starr cut him off.

"No."

"Because most people would be." Mr. Starr's voice was calm

and rational. "But we don't want to ruin your life. Ryder doesn't need a father."

Ryder flinched and wasn't sure that was the truth.

If Mr. Starr noticed, he didn't show it. "He just needs to save his mother's life, and if you *are* his father, I'd say you *owe* him that."

Thomas Trent inhaled sharply, held his breath, then let it out. "I'll have to talk to my agent first, and my lawyer. You'll be here, I assume?"

"Waiting for your call," Mr. Starr said.

Thomas Trent gave them a curt nod, then let himself out.

# 69

The phone call woke them up. Mr. Starr was lodged in his bed. Ryder had fallen asleep on top of the covers with the TV on. Outside, the lights from the city of Atlanta glowed in the blackness.

"Hello?" Ryder said into the phone, muting some show about great white sharks on Animal Planet.

"Is this Ryder?" Thomas Trent sounded exhausted, but the kind texture to his voice made Ryder ache to have this man really turn out to be his father.

"Yes." On the TV screen, a shark broke the water's surface, its rows of sharp teeth gushing blood.

"Okay, you and your . . . friend meet me tomorrow at the Pencil Building." Trent paused and cleared his throat. "Uh, it's 600 Peachtree. Take the elevator to the top. It's Troutman & Sanders. Ask for Leslie Spanko. She's my lawyer. We'll do the test there. You'll have to sign some things first."

Ryder heard a sudden shriek from the phone that wasn't Thomas Trent, but someone in the same room.

*"Is that him!"* The voice was sharp and hysterical.

Ryder heard the phone being covered and muffled talking and a stretch of silence before the phone was uncovered.

"Sorry," Trent said. "Just meet me there tomorrow at ten. Got that? Pencil Building. Top floor. Leslie Spanko. Okay? I gotta go."

*"What then?"* The second shriek was the last thing Ryder heard.

The line went dead and he sat there on the edge of his hotel bed with the phone in his hand and Mr. Starr lay on the other bed, blinking at him.

"Well?" Mr. Starr whispered.

"He's gonna do it," Ryder said. "Tomorrow."

Mr. Starr let out a long breath. "Well, good. This is very good, Ryder."

"How do you know?" Ryder's heart thumped against his ribs.

"This man is your father." Mr. Starr lay like a corpse, but his eyes flickered in the wavering blue light from the TV screen. "They're going to lock us down, but they'll give us what we need."

"Lock us down?" Ryder thought of the shrieking in the background of the phone.

"You're not going to be able to make any claims against him or his estate, but they'll give us the money we need for your mom."

"Mr. Starr, how do you know?" Ryder's voice trembled at the thought. They were so close, and he could really save his mother.

If Mr. Starr was right, this was it.

"Because I know. We'll have the money wired to New York and get this operation going. There's no reason to take chances. Then we'll catch the train back. Turn the TV off and get some sleep. Tomorrow is a big day."

Ryder did as he was told and got into bed, pulling the covers up to his chin, even though he knew he wouldn't sleep.

He could barely breathe.

## 70

*"I'm Ruby Shoesmith now." Ryder's mom smiled at Thomas Trent and the two of them hugged.*

*"Mom?" Ryder didn't think they knew he was there.*

*Trent wore a look of disbelief. "Not him."*

*"No," Ruby said. "Not him."*

*"Ryder," said a strange voice.*

*They were on the top of a skyscraper, at the edge, but when Ryder looked over he didn't see streets or buildings or traffic down below. He saw an angry, twisting ocean.*

*"Not you either." Thomas Trent was talking to Ryder's mom now. She wore her yellow puffy coat and her hair looked so black against it, like a traffic sign.*

*"Ryder," said the voice again.*

*Trent took her by the shoulders and threw her over the edge.*

*The great white shark just like the one from the Animal Planet*

*show broke through the water's surface like an angry missile, show-
ing nothing but teeth and blood.*

Ryder screamed and bolted upright in his bed.

"Ryder?" Mr. Starr said. "Easy. It's time. You've got to
help me up and get ready. I let you sleep, but we've got to get
moving."

Ryder shook the dream from his mind, but the sick feeling
remained. Outside it was cloudy and dark. The clock read 9:07.

Panic flooded Ryder's brain. "Mr. Starr? Can we make it?
Won't we have to get a connecting bus?"

"Easy, easy. We're gonna splurge and call a cab. We deserve
it. Now help me up."

Ryder helped Mr. Starr get ready, including wiping down
his upper body with a soapy washcloth and helping him put on
a clean shirt.

"Should I bring the baseball?" Ryder held it up.

"Absolutely. We need all the luck we can get," Mr. Starr
said.

Ryder fed Mr. Starr some oatmeal and a banana in the dining area, but he could eat nothing himself. His stomach crawled
with a strange mixture of excitement and horror. The dream
stayed fresh in his mind and he couldn't shake the heavy, dis-
mal feeling that something would go wrong.

His stomach said so, and so did the dark Atlanta sky as they
rode in the wheelchair-accessible Checker Cab into the city of
Atlanta. It took a few minutes to get Mr. Starr back out of the
cab and loaded into his chair. The driver was as cheerful and
friendly to them as some long-lost uncle. Even Mr. Starr lost his

grouchiness for a few moments in the face of the driver's brilliant, grinning teeth.

Ryder looked up at the towering building in front of them as he wheeled Mr. Starr up the reddish-brown granite ramp. He saw why they called it the Pencil—it was tall and thin and pointed, and stood alone, a good mile from the other skyscrapers clustered in the city's center. They rode the elevator up to the fifty-third floor and asked the woman at a polished wood reception desk for Leslie Spanko. She made a call and Leslie Spanko's assistant appeared, a young man who introduced himself as Giovanni Castiglione.

"You can call me Gio." The young man grinned at them and shrugged, then led them to a conference room as if he had no idea what was about to happen.

"Can I get you water or coffee?" Gio treated them the same as the cabdriver, like friends, but Ryder shook his head no. He couldn't drink anything. Mr. Starr stayed silent.

"I'll tell Ms. Spanko you're here," he said, still smiling.

One wall was all windows and it looked out across the suburbs of Atlanta to a huge low mountain hunkered down all alone in the middle of a flat sea of trees. Ryder parked Mr. Starr at the end of the table and sat down in the black leather chair closest to him.

"What's that?" Ryder pointed at the mountain.

A serious-looking woman with short red hair and glasses, wearing a dark gray pants suit, walked into the room and looked where Ryder was pointing. "Stone Mountain," she said. "It's the biggest single rock on the continent."

"It's a rock?"

"One big rock left by a glacier, all by its lonesome. Powerful, right?" The woman held out a long, cool hand for Ryder to shake, surprising him with her grip. "I'm Leslie."

Leslie turned to Mr. Starr, held out her hand, but retracted after a long moment of Mr. Starr's silent glare.

"I don't do handshakes," Mr. Starr said.

"That's fine." Leslie didn't seem to mind one bit. She sat down across the table from Ryder and set a file down in front of him before slapping down a chubby black-and-gold pen. "So, business."

"Where's your client?" Mr. Starr asked. "We're not doing this without him."

"Of course, of course." Leslie looked at her watch. "He tends to run late, but I wanted to explain the terms of the deal to you two anyway . . . in case you need to think about it. Now, are you the boy's guardian?"

"I am." Mr. Starr didn't hesitate to lie, but Ryder supposed that ultimately if Mr. Starr wasn't his guardian, then he didn't have one.

Ryder took the baseball out of his pocket and gripped it under the table.

"So, what we're proposing is a Genetic ID test that will give us 99.99 percent certainty of paternity." Leslie's face grew serious and her voice got lower. "However, the results will belong to us and we will sign an agreement stipulating that even though both sides take the test, neither can or will use it in a court of law to assert a paternity claim. In the event that the test does suggest paternity—and I repeat, my choice of words is *suggest*, we make no warrantees—then, based on that *possibility*, my client is willing to write you a one-time check for two hundred thousand dollars in exchange for a waiver that prevents any and all claims against him, his family, or his estate now and in the future."

Leslie stopped talking and looked from Mr. Starr to Ryder and back. "Understood?"

Silence filled the room. Ryder looked out at the enormous mountain of rock, all alone, just like him. This agreement would leave him that way. He had no idea about most of what she'd just said, but only kept thinking that if it meant they'd help his mom get well, he didn't care about any other parts of his crumbling dream. If he understood it right, it sounded to him as if part of the deal was Ryder being blocked from having anything to do with Thomas Trent, even if he was his son, and that hurt him deeply, more than he'd thought it would. He held the ball so tight, the joints in his fingers began to ache.

If all the mumbo jumbo they were talking about didn't end up helping his mom, he'd be like that big stone mountain outside the city, alone and lost.

# 71

Mr. Starr narrowed his eyes and disgust dripped from his voice. "So, if Ryder *isn't* Trent's son, we agree to go away, like we never existed. *But*, if he *is* Ryder's father, Trent pays for the mother's operation on the condition Ryder goes back to his own life for good and never tries to even contact Thomas Trent. How very nice."

"That is the deal." The lawyer frowned as if asking them not to blame the messenger.

"Ryder?" Mr. Starr asked.

"I . . . just care about my mom," Ryder said.

"Yes," Mr. Starr said. "We agree."

"Ryder?" Leslie's eyebrows appeared above the rims of her glasses. "Is that a 'yes'?"

"Yes," Ryder whispered.

The lawyer picked up the phone on the table and dialed

three numbers. "Gio? Yes, can you bring your notary stamp in here?"

Leslie hung up and turned to Mr. Starr. "I'm assuming you have a way to fix your signature."

"I do," Mr. Starr said. "Ryder can help me."

"Very good." Leslie took out the agreements. Gio came in and sat down beside her without a word. Leslie droned on with a bunch of therefores and whereases; Ryder lost count. When the room went silent again, Leslie Spanko held out the pen for Ryder to sign. He did, and then he helped Mr. Starr sign below where it said "Guardian."

Leslie tilted her head back and studied the agreements through the bottoms of her glasses before she nodded and looked at Giovanni. "Gio, would you ask Mr. Trent to come in, please."

Gio got up with a nod and disappeared.

Thomas Trent entered with dark bags under his moist green eyes and needing a shave. He wore a suit, but the shirt had an open collar and the buttons were off so that the collar jutted up on one side toward his ear. He looked at Ryder and nodded, then signed the papers without sitting down.

A nurse came in next with a box that she opened, removing some paperwork, small plastic capsules, and cotton swabs she laid down on a white hand towel beside the box. "Okay, who's first?"

Leslie Spanko smiled at her client. "Thomas?"

The nurse put on rubber gloves and asked Thomas Trent to open his mouth. She took four swabs and wiped them at the same time on the inside of his cheek, then placed two into one capsule and two in another. Gio pulled out a chair for Thomas Trent. The pitcher sat down and so did Gio.

Instead of swabbing Ryder right away, she sealed Thomas Trent's capsules with stickers before signing across them, then inserting them into smaller boxes along with paperwork she filled out and had Thomas Trent sign as well.

Finally, she circled the table and swabbed Ryder's cheeks. It didn't hurt. Thomas Trent just sat there, staring at Ryder with the sad, eager look of someone studying a jigsaw puzzle that was missing just one piece. The nurse sealed and signed the capsules. Ryder signed the box and the paperwork with Mr. Starr adding his assisted scrawl.

The nurse packed everything back up in the box and looked up at them all. "I'll ship this out and we'll know within a day."

Everyone sat so quiet, Ryder could hear the soft wheeze of Mr. Starr's breathing.

That's when the conference room door was flung open, banging the wall, and a tall woman with blond hair and lots of makeup burst into the room.

*"You stop right there and give me that box!"*

It was the same shriek Ryder had heard over the phone.

The woman didn't wait, but instead snatched the box from the nurse's hands before anyone could say a word.

## 72

The woman's pale blue eyes were so red and swollen it looked to Ryder like she'd been in a fight. She wore high heels and tight white pants with a gold jacket over a black silk blouse. Gold and diamonds sparkled from her wrists, neck, and ears. Even with swollen eyes she was so beautiful, there was something unreal about her.

She clutched the box and glared at Thomas Trent. "You'd do this to me? You'd do this to your *children?*"

Thomas Trent grabbed his lower jaw and sputtered. "I . . . it's what's right. If he's mine, I have to help. Don't you see that?"

*"If he's yours?"* The shriek went up so high Giovanni covered his ears. "Look at him! He's a street urchin! Look! Look at this *monster!*"

No one could help following the point of her finger at Mr. Starr.

"This is a *circus*! A *freak show*! It's a scam, Thomas. They want your *money*. Everyone told you that, but no, you have to be that swell guy. What about your *family*!"

"Brooke, please." Thomas Trent sounded desperate.

"Please? Don't you please me!" Brooke Trent stamped a foot. "Some strumpet from the past and she never *tells you*? You either come with me and our children or you can start over with this . . . this *lost boy* and his monster. You won't have both, Thomas. That I promise you."

Thomas Trent looked at his wife for a moment, then he turned toward Ryder.

## 73

The famous ballplayer stared with trembling lips at Ryder until a single tear slipped down his cheek and dripped from his chin.

"I'm sorry." Thomas Trent spoke in barely a whisper, and then he was gone, with his wife, and the box.

Leslie Spanko cleared her throat. The nurse and Gio struggled to wipe the horror from their faces.

Mr. Starr exhaled loudly, then clucked his tongue. "Monster."

Ryder exploded from his seat and raced for the door.

"Ryder!" Mr. Starr yelled, but Ryder kept going.

He burst through the glass doors just as the elevator closed. Ryder punched the down button and paced three times before a *ting* brought another car. He jumped in and punched the lobby button with his finger, over and over, until the door closed. The elevator swooped down, then stopped at forty and yet again at twenty-three. Ryder fumed and jiggled and told himself if his car stopped, theirs might have too.

The lighted numbers counted down from 10 to L and Ryder positioned himself in front of the doors with the baseball out of his pocket again and held tightly in his hand. The doors started to open. He squeezed through and ran full speed for the set of huge brass-framed glass doors in a great archway just as they swallowed up Thomas Trent and his wife. Ryder jostled several people. A woman screamed. A man yelled and grabbed at his shirt. Ryder slapped his hand away and kept going.

He hit the door at a run and pushed through. He went left, down a set of granite stairs and saw them getting into the Maserati, parked crookedly right there on the street with its hazard lights blinking.

Ryder shouted. "Trent!"

Thomas Trent turned in disbelief.

"You get in this car!" His wife's shrieking command made everyone around stop and stare.

Ryder held the baseball up in the air so Trent could see it. The big league pitcher seemed hypnotized by the ball, so Ryder kept it up high as he marched toward him, hoping, praying, counting on its magic.

Thomas Trent's mouth opened and closed without words. Ryder circled the long blue hood of the car that cost more than his mother's operation.

"Here." Ryder put the ball right in Thomas Trent's face.

Trent winced, and grabbed hold of the ball instinctively. He held it in his hand, turning it this way and that, reading the words.

"I read your letter," Ryder said. "The one you wrote to my mom when you were with her."

Thomas Trent tilted his head in confusion, then a light went on and Ryder knew he remembered the letter.

Without even knowing that he'd memorized it, Ryder repeated the words Thomas Trent had written thirteen years ago. *"Nothing could make me stop loving you, and so I always will."*

Thomas Trent stared, amazed.

Ryder's heart swelled. He felt the magic and knew everything Doyle had said about being positive and everything Mr. Starr said about the luck the ball contained was true. The wife's ranting in the street was like a crow's, insistent and annoying, but without any real impact, just empty noise. This man, who he knew was his father, couldn't resist the truth of it, the truth of the ball, his own words written so carefully, his love for his gem, Ruby, and for the lost boy who belonged to them both.

# 74

Thomas Trent heard the cawing of his wife.

Ryder saw his eyes dart past and lock onto her hysterical tirade as she shouted and waved her arms and danced in place.

"No." Trent handed the ball back to Ryder. "I can't. It's yours."

"No." Ryder swung his head from left to right and folded his arms, refusing to take it.

"That wasn't me," Trent said.

"Liar! You said you *loved* her! You're a *liar*!"

"Take it." Trent held it out to him, shaking it.

"No!" Ryder screamed.

*"Thomas! Right now!"* The wife screamed louder.

Trent huffed and sidestepped Ryder with a glare. He wound up and fired the ball, pitching it at the granite wall of the skyscraper.

The ball exploded against the wall, cracking like a rifle shot.

Ryder spun and watched it drop to the concrete, where it lay like roadkill. He heard the car doors slam and the engine whine. Before he could move, the car was gone in a whoosh of hot air.

In a trance, Ryder walked over to the ball and picked it up.

The seam had split open and the brittle leather skin hung limp from the tightly bound wool strands within, brown and dusty and crumbling with rot. Ryder put it in his pocket anyway and walked in a daze, back into the building and up the elevator. He walked right into the law offices and back into the conference room where they all still remained. He sat down, but before anyone could speak, the phone on the conference table rang.

Leslie Spanko picked it up and talked in single words. "Yes . . . Mmm . . . No . . . Yes . . . Yes . . . Okay."

Spanko hung up and looked at Mr. Starr. "The Trents are offering you ten thousand dollars."

"For what?" Mr. Starr asked.

Leslie Spanko thought for a moment. "To end all this. To go away."

Mr. Starr sucked on his tongue. "No. You can tell them we don't need ten thousand dollars. We need *two hundred thousand*. She can take that ten thousand and shove it right up her nose."

"Mr. Starr . . ." Ryder was floating again. He'd felt like this so much in the past week that he began to hope it all really *was* a dream. He just needed to wake up.

But the feel of the desk's smooth surface beneath his sweaty palms and the sniff from Gio as he and the nurse got up, leaving them alone with the lawyer, and the click of the latch on the door let Ryder know it wasn't a dream and he wasn't going to just wake up.

"No," Mr. Starr said. "Get me out of here, Ryder. It's over."

"But you said . . ."

*"I said it's over!"*

Mr. Starr's shriek was as hysterical and jolting as Brooke Trent's had been. Ryder got up and took hold of the chair. Leslie Spanko opened the door without speaking and escorted them to the elevator.

"I'm sorry," the lawyer said with somber sincerity as she held the door so they could get in.

Then, the elevator doors closed on her face and they plummeted down.

# 75

They took a bus back to their hotel and packed their belongings. They headed to the train station and spent all afternoon there before getting on the Crescent line for New York City at 8:04 p.m. Mr. Starr didn't speak. Ryder kept quiet too. There was nothing to say.

Without a word, Ryder helped Mr. Starr from the bathroom into his bed, then tucked the destroyed baseball into his duffel bag, climbed into his own bunk, and fell asleep to the clacking sway of the train. In the morning they ate bagels wrapped in cellophane from the dining car and Ryder tore the metallic covers off of plastic containers of orange juice. Ryder then lay back in his bunk and stared out the window at the world sweeping by. He wondered several times whether or not he could get outside the train and simply jump when they crossed one of the bridges through the mountains of Virginia, but it was just a thought. He never even got out of the bunk except to eat a sandwich in the afternoon and use the bathroom.

In New Jersey, the skyline of New York City suddenly appeared on the horizon and Ryder had no idea what he'd do when he got home besides go to the hospital and stare at his mom and pray for a miracle. He didn't believe in miracles. He'd never seen one and he didn't understand how people could believe in something—truly believe—if they hadn't seen it for themselves. Still, he'd try because it was all he had left. He wasn't even going to think about Doyle and the money he was trying to raise. Ryder knew now that Mr. Starr was right. Doyle wasn't for real even if he had a good heart. Doyle was a wild dreamer.

And Ryder didn't need wild dreams about FDNY fund-raising on Twitter. He needed a good old-fashioned the-doctors-have-never-seen-anything-like-it miracle.

He cried, too. A lot. He kept his face buried in the foam pillow so Mr. Starr didn't have to listen. He knew adults didn't want to hear that kind of thing and he appreciated everything Mr. Starr had done, even if he'd been wrong, even if they came up short.

It wasn't Mr. Starr's fault, after all. It was Ryder's alone. He replayed the moments over in the park, right before the accident, the things he'd been angry about: his mom pushing him to make friends, him using the excuse of being poor and not having a phone, her throwing her lowly job in his face, and him insulting her with the idea that he'd grow up and become someone like Thomas Trent. He now knew that meant valuing cars and houses more than people's lives.

Then he remembered pulling back from her, and her pulling him too, only she slipped and got hit by a car, breaking her ribs and leg and smashing her heart so that it would fail any day now and all he could do was watch and wait.

Everything went dark.

Ryder cried out.

The train whooshed through the tunnel beneath the Hudson River.

Ryder wondered what it would be like to have the tunnel collapse. They'd all be crushed by a million tons of water, concrete, and mud.

He wished for that. That was something that wouldn't take a miracle, just another tragedy, another human error in calculation, or driving . . . or a stupid angry response.

Ryder climbed down in the darkness and vomited his sandwich into the stainless steel bowl of their toilet.

"You okay?" Mr. Starr asked.

Ryder washed his face and hands and went back into their compartment. "You're talking to me now?"

"You yelled when we went in the tunnel. Why?"

Ryder didn't even want to get into it, but he felt obligated. "I was thinking about all the things, every little thing that I could have done different on that day."

"The day of the accident?" Mr. Starr asked.

"I could have pushed instead of pulled. I could have made a joke instead of a jab. I could have . . . I don't know, not hit a home run."

"Home run?"

Ryder sighed.

268

"Tell me about that. Tell me all the things leading up to when she got hurt." Mr. Starr lay still. Even his eyes were motionless.

"Why?" Ryder asked.

"Just tell me." Even his voice seemed not to move. "I think it'll help."

Ryder did tell. He described that day, the park, his teammates and friends, hitting that home run, even falling in the muddy grass and looking up at the clouds with his mom. He wished so badly he could go back. Telling it didn't make him feel any better and he said so.

"I know," Mr. Starr said. "I've been thinking about everything, too."

"About how she's gonna die?"

The train groaned and swayed and thumped the tracks.

"Yes," he said. "About how she's gonna die."

## 76

They arrived at Penn Station, and Doyle picked them up. He helped Mr. Starr home and then took Ryder to the hospital.

Mr. Starr stayed in his apartment. Ryder and Doyle passed Ashleigh Love hurrying up the stairs with fresh supplies slung over her shoulder, fretting out loud about them being gone too long. Ryder said nothing, he just followed Doyle and climbed up into the passenger seat of Derek Raymer's truck that Doyle had on loan.

Doyle was talking, fast. Ryder had a hard time paying attention to all the Twitter fund-raising talk.

"How much?" Ryder asked, his heart stung by a faint pang of hope.

"Well, forty-seven thousand." Doyle stopped at a light, glancing over at him with a worried look. "But, you know, we're just one huge retweet away from this thing exploding, right?"

Ryder sighed. "I don't even know what that means, Doyle."

"A retweet." Doyle turned the truck. "Like someone like Carlos Beltran or Eli Manning or maybe Michael Strahan or Diane Sawyer takes my tweet and then tweets it out to *their* followers. They have millions. Then all of a sudden, the money comes pouring in at a really fast rate."

"So, all you need is a retweet." Ryder couldn't help sounding bitter, almost bored.

Doyle nodded his head viciously, like a loyal dog.

They pulled up to the hospital and parked in the garage. They crossed the street and entered, people coming and going with no idea Ryder's mom was about to die. He hated them and their smiles and the one who held the door for them. He hated everyone and everything and each step closer to his mother's room he hated them more and his limbs got heavier and heavier.

The doctor was in there and the look on his face startled Ryder, heaping more fear onto his heart.

"How is she?" Doyle asked.

The doctor looked at Ryder, then Doyle, and spoke very low. "Her heartbeat is irregular and the pressure is starting to drop. Maybe a few more days. I'm sorry."

The doctor went out. Doyle pulled out his phone and started to tweet, thumbs skipping over the screen in a blur, like he could somehow tweet her back to life. Doyle clenched his jaw so tight that the muscles in his cheek did a quiet dance. Ryder felt the tears coursing down his own cheeks again. He went to the bed and spread his arms over his mother, pressing his face into the hair piled around her neck. A sob tore free from his chest.

*"Mommmmmm!"*

## 77

Doyle let him cry for a while before he tapped him on the back and said they should probably go. Ryder was exhausted again and he let Doyle direct him out to the truck. He climbed the steps of their apartment building slowly. They met Ashleigh on the third floor, heading down at a slow, steady pace.

They seemed to startle her. "Oh, I better give you two my number. I don't think the night nurse is scheduled to come until tomorrow. You can call if you need me in the night."

"The night?" Ryder asked. "What do you mean?"

Ashleigh nodded. "He's not good. I gave him some penicillin, but in his condition . . ."

"What's wrong?" Doyle asked.

She huffed. "I told him. You can't just go away without a nurse. He has a shunt in his intestines that has to be taken care of. The old fool. Must have hurt like I don't know what. He said he didn't have time for that. I don't believe that for a second."

She stared at Ryder and he bit the edge of his lower lip because he had no idea Mr. Starr wasn't well or that he was in that kind of pain.

"Well." Ashleigh shook her head and started down the stairs. "He's on the computer now. Wouldn't listen to me when I said he needs some sleep. If you can get him to do that, he might not end up in the hospital."

"Hospital?" Ryder said.

"His fever is a hundred and one." She spoke up at them from the landing below. "Any higher and that's where he'll be, even if I have to get an elephant gun to sedate him."

Ryder and Doyle looked at each other and started to climb without saying anything. When they got to the top, Ryder saw light bleeding underneath Mr. Starr's door.

Ryder didn't say anything, he just walked past his own apartment door and knocked at Mr. Starr's.

"Leave me alone!" Mr. Starr's shout echoed down the empty stairwell.

"Mr. Starr?" Ryder shouted through the door. "Are you okay? It's me, Ryder! And Doyle!"

"I'm working! Go!"

Doyle's mouth twisted into a look of disgust. "Everything *sounds* normal anyway, the old grump."

"She said 'hospital.'" Ryder frowned.

"That's if the fever keeps going up," Doyle said. "He'll be fine. He's on medicine now. That'll fix him up."

Ryder nodded, but left reluctantly. When he swung open the door to his apartment he was again moved by the smells that made it seem like his mother would be walking out of the bedroom any second to greet them. He turned on the lights, but everything was quiet and the shattered pieces of the blue-and-white porcelain lamp still lay on the floor.

"Yeah." Doyle looked at the mess too. "Got a dustpan? I can help you clean that up."

There was a broom and dustpan in the narrow closet next to the fridge and Ryder took them out. Together, he and Doyle cleaned up the lamp.

"How about something to eat?" Doyle clapped his hands, his voice upbeat. "Can I help you put something together? You want to maybe grab something at a diner?"

Ryder looked around at the empty apartment. "What's going to happen to me?"

"Well . . . uh . . . Let's not go negative, right?" Doyle took out his phone and began tapping its face. "We got . . . look, another nine hundred and eighty-seven dollars in just this past hour."

"He said *two days, Doyle!*" Ryder was furious. "Don't you *get* it!"

"I know, but things could happen . . . like I said, a retweet could—"

*"Get out!"*

In the silence that followed, Ryder heard ringing in his ears from his own scream.

"Leave me alone, Doyle." Ryder's voice was lifeless.

"Yeah, well, you need some sleep, bud. I get it. You get some rest. I'll stop back and check on you tomorrow. You got my number."

"I got your number."

"Okay, well . . ." Doyle started for the door.

"Doyle? I'm sorry," Ryder said. "Thank you. For everything."

"You got it, kid." Doyle stroked his mustache and closed the door behind him.

Ryder stumbled to the bedroom, lay down on his mother's bed with the smell of her all around him, and plunged into a dark sleep.

# 78

Ryder woke with a bowling ball in his stomach. The hurt made him heavy and dull. He had no idea what his life was about to become. In a strange way, he didn't care. In a life without his mom, nothing would matter.

He got up and wandered into the tiny kitchen to sit on the floor.

Ryder didn't know how long he sat, but when Doyle knocked on the door it was ten thirty. Ryder let him in, but Doyle was there to take him to the hospital. Ryder nodded and quickly changed and got his coat.

Out in the hallway, Doyle nodded toward Mr. Starr's door. "We should probably check in on him, no?"

Ryder nodded, shuffled down the hall, and knocked.

"Working!" Mr. Starr cried out from inside. He didn't sound angry anymore, but Ryder wondered if that was because he was sick.

"Do you need anything?" Ryder hollered.

"Working!"

Doyle sighed and shook his head. "The morning nurse probably came. He sounds fine, Ryder."

"What work?" Ryder shook his head too. He supposed this was the end of Mr. Starr. He was obviously washing his hands of the situation. He'd done his best, Ryder had to admit that, but now it was over. Mr. Starr was going back to his life, whatever life that was. Ryder thought it strange how the whole thing with Thomas Trent didn't even seem real. It was like the accident itself, or the shark dream with him and his mom on top of the skyscraper in the ocean. Crazy. Impossible.

"Come on." Doyle led the way down the stairs.

They went to the hospital and sat with his mom. She didn't move. Her skin was losing its color and Ryder imagined he heard the beeps of the machines slowing down, their rhythm off, although he wasn't sure. Doyle had serious conversations with the staff about Ryder outside in the hallway. Ryder heard him invoking FDNY over and over again, but Ryder's sense was that the time for him to be plugged into the system was coming soon. They'd get him.

He considered that in a distant way, as if it were happening to a character in a movie. The boy would go through the courts. The fireman would watch over him, but despite the best of intentions, the system would win. The boy would end up in a detention center, or maybe a foster home, both grim places to be. The boy would grow up, empty and cold, alone and lost.

Ryder shrugged and sighed and touched his mother's face.

The tears were gone, anyway. He was empty. It was evening already, the sun setting somewhere beyond the buildings outside the hospital window, and it was time to go.

Doyle had a night shift to get to, but he insisted they stop at a diner because Ryder had to eat. Doyle actually got him to swallow three spoonfuls of tomato soup along with two bites of a grilled cheese before depositing him in the apartment. Ryder lay down on his mother's bed and slept.

Ryder slept a long time and woke to the sound of screaming and pounding.

*"Ryder! Ryder!"*

POUND. POUND. POUND.

*"Ryder!"*

Ryder jumped up, his heart strangling him because he somehow knew it was news that his mother had passed. What else could it be?

He dashed past the living room widow, which was letting in the morning sun, and to their apartment door and flung it open.

Mr. Starr sat crookedly in his chair; the silver travel coffee mug he'd used to bang the door hung loose from one twisted hand.

"Ryder!" Mr. Starr looked horrible, pale and drooping, but his eyes glowed. "We might have it! We just might *have* it!"

"Mr. Starr? Have what?"

"The way to *save her.*"

278

# 79

Mr. Starr tightened his lips when Ryder asked him to explain. "No. I don't want to jinx it. Get your coat. You're going with me. I need you there."

Ryder grabbed his coat. The spark of hope glowed faint in the cold ashes of his heart, too weak to really stir him. Still, he knew how to obey his elders. Ryder pocketed his keys and the TracFone and began to close the door behind him.

"Wait," Mr. Starr said. "The ball. Do you have the ball?"

"Mr. Starr, that ball isn't worth anything. There's no luck in that ball."

"Get the ball." Mr. Starr's voice didn't allow any argument.

Ryder went back inside, fished the wrecked baseball out of the duffel bag he'd yet to unpack, stuffed it into his coat pocket, and left.

Ryder wheeled Mr. Starr to the service elevator and down

the wobbly ramp in the back, then out onto the street.

"Subway. B train. Downtown. Let's go." Mr. Starr's voice quavered with excitement, even through his grumpy tone.

They took the B to Rockefeller Center, got on the elevator, went up, and came out on Sixth Avenue.

"Fifth and Fifty-Seventh," Mr. Starr said.

Ryder crossed Sixth Avenue and headed down Forty-Ninth Street. He couldn't even imagine where they were headed. When they got to Fifth Avenue, Ryder couldn't help looking up at the majestic buildings, home to the fanciest stores, banks, and offices in the world. This was the center of the city, where the elite, rich, and famous came to work and play. He couldn't help thinking of Thomas and Brooke Trent. This was their kind of territory.

His throat grew tight.

They came to a gold-gilt entrance with twisty columns, lanterns, and three alcoves above the doorway with golden statues of ladies from three hundred years ago. The gold letters said it was THE CROWN BUILDING. Next to the fancy entrance stood stores with signs that said PIAGET and BULGARI. Ryder looked up and saw that the buildings here disappeared into the blue and cloudy sky.

"Mr. Starr? Here?"

"Yes. Go in."

There were men in black-and-gold livery uniforms at the desk just inside the brass-framed glass doors.

"Esther Newberg." Mr. Starr spoke with authority.

The man's eyes widened at the sight of Mr. Starr, but he looked away and said, "ICM, third floor."

"I know it's ICM, you twit."

Ryder gave the man an apologetic look and wheeled Mr. Starr to the elevators. When the doors closed, Ryder whispered, "Who's Esther Newberg? What's ICM?"

"She's a literary agent. It's a talent agency, although with some of the clients they represent I find the word to have very little meaning."

"Mr. Starr, why are we here? I really just want to go back to the hospital to see my mom."

"You'll know why." The doors opened and Ryder wheeled him off.

They passed through the wide opening in a smoky glass wall that enclosed a waiting area, reception desk, and a chrome set of stairs leading up to the next floor.

"Esther Newberg," Mr. Starr barked at the receptionist.

She didn't flinch. "Are you Mr. Starr?"

"No, I'm the other twisted wreck of a man on her schedule this morning."

The woman smiled, and it was genuine. "I'll tell her you're here."

An assistant named Zoe came down the stairs and took them up the elevator, using a card to access the fourth floor. It was quiet and uncomfortable in the elevator. Ryder wasn't excited, only confused and annoyed.

"Esther says you used to write for the *Post*." Zoe wore a short purple dress and had her long hair pulled back.

"And, considering her love affair with the *Times*, I suppose I should be grateful for the audience." Mr. Starr just couldn't help being a grouch.

"She says you're very talented, that's all." Zoe smiled.

"We were just talking about the dubious use of that word," Mr. Starr said.

The doors opened and Zoe led them to a large corner office. Behind a massive desk that faced out from two walls of windows looking out onto the park as well as the Hudson River sat a tiny woman with short reddish hair and dark blazing eyes that seemed like they could mean life or death, depending on her mood. She was made up with a bit of lipstick and mascara and wore a single strand of pearls against an elegant black dress.

"Well," Esther said, not affected in the least by Mr. Starr's appearance, or the presence of a twelve-year-old boy. "You've grown older, Stephen."

Mr. Starr snorted. "And crooked."

Esther huffed impatiently and puckered her lips. "You were never straight, Stephen; it's what I liked about you."

Esther's mouth curled into a small smile. Her eyes glimmered with mischief and shifted to Ryder. "And this is *him*?"

"It is. Show her the ball, Ryder."

Ryder was totally confused. He'd forgotten about the ball, but as he reached into his coat pocket, he realized that besides having shelves and counters covered with books he guessed had been written by her clients, Esther Newberg had signed baseballs and photos of players and managers all over the place. Most of them looked like they had something to do with the Red Sox.

He handed her the ball across the wide desk.

She took it and turned it in her hand, frowning at the torn seams, but examining the signatures before setting it down in front of her. "Very good, Stephen."

Another ball on the desk had caught Ryder's attention and Esther saw him looking at it.

"You know what that one is?" she asked. "Go ahead, pick it up."

Ryder lifted the ball off its stand. It was fresh and new and it had a World Series logo on it. "What?"

"Game six. Green Monster. Foul ball. Know how I got it?"

Ryder shook his head and replaced the ball in its stand.

"Fell right into my lap." She glanced at Mr. Starr. "Seriously. Bounced twice. I didn't even move. That's fate, right? That's life, isn't it?"

"So . . ." Esther picked up a thin stack of paper and let it drop beside the ball, her voice changing to signal that this was business. "People are interested. . . . These days no one's buying outlines with a few sample chapters, but in your case, with your background, I think we might be able to do something. Probably not what you want, but *something*."

"Not what I want?" Mr. Starr sounded like he was trying to contain some anger.

Esther shook her head. "To really cash in on this, I need to have the whole thing, Stephen. People will be able to sink their teeth into it then, and I can get you some real money."

"They can't have the whole thing!" Mr. Starr startled Ryder, but Esther Newberg didn't even blink.

"Why not, Stephen?" Esther delivered the question as a challenge.

"It'll take me six months, *a year* if I take the time I should. I can't wait six months. I can't wait one. I need this *today*,

283

Esther!" Mr. Starr was breathing hard and Ryder remembered Ashleigh Love's warning about his health. "I'm . . . I don't mean to be so abrupt."

"Abrupt works with me." Esther was unfazed. "I think I can get you a couple hundred thousand for this . . . but you've got to finish it."

"Esther," Mr. Starr sounded tired and sad, "I need the money now. Today."

Esther touched the thin stack of paper on her desk. "That part's all true? The mother? The operation?"

"It's why I'm *doing* this." Mr. Starr stared and a single tear rolled down his face. "I can save her. I have to . . . I need two hundred thousand, but I need it *now*."

Esther took a breath and held it before letting it out. She gave a curt nod, held up a finger, and picked up her phone.

"Zoe, get me Lindsey Frost." Esther turned her chair toward the window, looking out over the budding trees of Central Park and the row of skyscrapers it seemed to hold at bay. "Lindsey? Good. I can give it to you, but not for fifty. I've got seventy-five on the table from someone else, but I need two hundred and I need it right now. . . . Well, you're the one who said it's a bestseller, not me, and Tearsten Casanova thinks the same thing and I'm calling her next unless you give me two hundred. . . . I don't care how business is done these days, Lindsey. I have a deal and I *will* sell it today because I *have* to sell it today and I've got enough buyers that I'm not worried. It's just that I thought of you before anyone and you can see why. If it's beyond you, then let me go. . . . No, eighty is not two hundred, Lindsey. . . . You're way off. . . . No, that's fine."

Esther hung up the phone. "That didn't go very well."

Mr. Starr's tongue crept out of his mouth and worked the edges of his lips. "Can you get two hundred from the other person?"

Esther looked at him hard. "If I can't get two hundred from Lindsey, I can't get it from anyone, Stephen. She wants this, but it's a tough market right now. You don't even have a finished book."

Mr. Starr made a gurgling noise. The phone buzzed. Esther hit the speaker.

"Esther?" It was Zoe's voice. "I've got Lindsey Frost on line two."

Esther's eyes twinkled. She pursed her lips and picked up the phone. "Lindsey? Talk to me."

# 80

The agent listened, her face giving nothing away.

Ryder held his breath.

He couldn't believe this was happening. He'd given up hope, but now it was alive. Mr. Starr was right, they were so close, but they'd been close before with Thomas Trent, and Ryder wondered what this book was and what it would mean for the Trents. He doubted it could be anything good.

Finally, Esther took a breath and said, "I told you, two hundred, Lindsey. Why are we wasting each other's time? Tearsten Casanova already offered me seventy-five and that was before she knew *you* wanted it too. . . ."

Esther winked at them. "Well, I don't care about your board. Your board won't complain when this thing becomes a bestseller. There aren't a lot of stories like this out there. You know that. . . ."

Esther listened and then she bit her lip and scowled. "Hang on, Lindsey."

Esther covered the phone and her eyes bored into Mr. Starr. "I've got her up to a hundred, Stephen. Do you want me to take it or not?"

"It's not what we *need*, Esther. Keep going. Get more."

Esther's look got even darker. "I'm telling you that without the whole book this is the absolute *best* you're going to get, Stephen. Tearsten Casanova wants it, but she hates unfinished manuscripts and she said seventy-five was her final and when she says 'final,' she means it. This is the best we are going to get, so, take it or leave it."

"You're *sure*, Esther?" Her name barely escaped Mr. Starr's twisted lips.

"I'm sorry," she whispered, shaking her head.

"Then tell her no."

"No?"

"*No.* Come on, Ryder. Let's get out of here." Mr. Starr jammed his hand against the controller and the chair jerked awkwardly toward the door.

"Stephen . . ." Esther stood up.

"No," Mr. Starr said, "it's not your fault. I know you did your best. We have to go."

Ryder followed, glancing back at the agent.

Zoe stuck her head in the doorway. "Esther, I've got Caroline Kennedy on line two."

Esther Newberg shook her head sadly, sighed, and picked up the phone. "Caroline?"

Mr. Starr navigated his chair through the desks to the

elevator. Ryder got on with him, dazed and unable to even think.

"Why didn't you take the money?" he asked as the car dropped toward the ground.

"I promised myself that if I ever wrote a book, it'd have a happy ending, not like this. Not like me. The world doesn't need another tragedy." Mr. Starr stared hard at him. "I'm not writing that book."

Ryder started to cry.

"I'm sorry, Ryder." Mr. Starr's voice was tattered with pain.

Ryder sniffed and tried not to sob. "I never had a father, and now it's like I've got two. You and Doyle, but now it's too late."

The elevator stopped. The bell rang as the doors opened. Mr. Starr buzzed out into the lobby without a word. Ryder held the door open and they were out on the street, people streaming by in the kaleidoscope of his tears. They had no idea how sick he was with grief.

"What now?" Ryder whispered.

"Now?" Mr. Starr let out a ragged sigh, his voice cracking. "We go say good-bye."

# 81

Ryder didn't think the machines hooked up to his mother could sound any slower, any weaker.

Doyle sat tucked into the corner, just looking at Ryder's mom. Ryder knew it was her, but if someone had showed him a picture like this three weeks ago he would never have believed it was his mom. His mom glowed with life. She bubbled with it.

Now her parted lips were dry and motionless beneath the oxygen tubes snaked into her nose. Her hair lay matted, greasy, and lifeless; gone was its luster and bounce. He felt so tired he wanted to just lie down beside her, go to sleep, and never wake up.

Mr. Starr bumped into the backs of his legs with the wheelchair and softly apologized. Ryder made room for him. He didn't know what else he could do but stand there and look. Doyle cleared his throat, stood, and gripped Ryder's shoulder.

Ryder looked up at him, tears streaming silently down his cheeks. "Can't we do anything? There has to be *something*."

Doyle's mustache drooped to his chin. He swallowed and looked over at Mr. Starr with red and weary eyes. Mr. Starr ignored them both. He navigated his chair alongside the bed, awkwardly leaned forward and sideways, raised an arm, and let his mangled hand drag its fingers across her cheek.

He whispered something. It was more than a good-bye, or a long good-bye; then he settled back into the chair and reversed it toward the foot of the bed.

Ryder suddenly knew what he had to do.

He slipped free from Doyle's grip and moved a chair next to her bed. He sat down and took her hand in both of his, twining their fingers. Then he rested his head on the bed so that he could watch the rise and fall of her chest. He would stay there and hold her hand and watch, until the very end. He knew no one could take him away from this spot. No one could separate them . . . until she was gone.

Time crawled. Nurses and doctors came and went, talking in low voices that floated behind him, ghostlike in the sterile room.

Ryder drifted in and out of sleep, the slow steady sound of the heart monitor lulling him, and the exhaustion of it all coaxing him under for five or ten minutes at a time. When he wasn't sleeping, he was praying. He couldn't help that. He thought it was what she'd want.

When the voices rose to a sudden high pitch, he jerked

awake. His heart sprinted in panic. The beeping? Was it gone? The noise. The hurry. The commotion.

Doyle lifted him up and away and he struggled, kicking and screaming and crying. "No! No! No!"

## 82

They picked her up and laid her onto a white gurney. There were five of them, rushing, frantic, shouting.

Ryder shrieked, but his shrill cry was lost in the noise, and then she was gone.

"No! No! No!"

Doyle held him tight, so tight he grew faint from want of air. "Ryder, no. Stop. Please."

"They *took* her! She's *gone!*" The agony tore him in half, his eyes desperately searching the empty space she'd disappeared through.

The doorway grew suddenly dark with the tall figure of a man. Ryder choked at the sight of him.

Thomas Trent wore a dark leather jacket and a somber face. He looked like he needed some sleep and a shave. His green eyes were red-rimmed and puffy. "They're going to try and save her, Ryder."

Thomas Trent let his words sink in before he continued. "I'm sorry you had to wait."

"What?" Ryder knew it was a dream.

It was like the shark dream, so real, so horribly real.

But Thomas Trent crossed the threshold, stepped into the room, and placed a strong hand alongside Ryder's face. Trent's fingers curled around the cord of muscle in the back of Ryder's neck.

"I said, 'I'm sorry you had to wait.' It wasn't right. I . . . it's hard to explain. I won't even try. But you were right. I lied. I *did* love her. Part of me still does. . . ."

Ryder was afraid to even ask, but he had to. "Can they save her?"

"I think they can." Thomas Trent smiled weakly. "I wanted to tell you, in person. I had to do this, but now I have to go. I won't ask you to understand that either, but this is the last time you'll see me, Ryder. There won't be any more money, and I can't be a father to you."

"I . . ." Ryder's eyes blurred with tears. "I don't *care.*"

Ryder laughed and cried and he hugged Thomas Trent tightly before letting him go. The big league player looked like he might cry too, but he bit his lip and nodded at Mr. Starr and Doyle, then turned and walked out the door.

# 83

Darkness filled the window of his mother's hospital room by the time the doctor came in later that night.

Ryder jumped up. So did Doyle. Mr. Starr jerked awake and straightened in his chair.

"She's very strong," the doctor said. "I feel pretty safe saying she's going to make it."

They whooped and hugged the doctor. Mr. Starr beamed up at them from his chair and they hugged him too. Then Doyle picked Ryder up and spun him around. The doctor laughed and excused himself and said Ryder's mom would be in recovery for another hour or so.

They talked and laughed and Ryder glowed with a joy whose warmth and depth he could never explain. Finally, each of them settled quietly into his own thoughts. Ryder studied his hands, thinking of all he'd seen and done—Yankee Stadium,

Atlanta, the batting contest, the Braves' locker room, the lawyers' offices, and then the literary agent. He looked up to see Mr. Starr staring warmly at him with that odd smile of his.

"What?" Ryder asked.

"I was thinking . . . about happy endings." Mr. Starr's eyes twinkled.

"Are you going to write it now?" Ryder asked.

Mr. Starr only chuckled.

# ONE YEAR LATER . . .

In Central Park, birds chattered and sang in the trees behind the bleachers. Ryder turned his face up to the sun, soaking up its warmth and marshaling his concentration. He opened his eyes and blinked at the batter. His team had two outs. It was the bottom of the final inning, but the winning run stood bouncing atop the third base bag. When the batter stepped into the box, the runner stretched his legs, leaning toward home, then taking a four-foot lead.

Ryder punched his glove and coiled his muscles, ready for anything.

The pitcher wound up and sent one low toward the inside corner of the plate. The batter swung and a crack exploded into the sunshine and the breeze. Ryder sprang from his spot, leaping into the air without the shred of a thought. The ball sounded off against the pocket of his glove like a rifle shot.

The stands erupted. His team jumped into the air, hooting and hollering and swarming toward him. He stood and let them swamp him with hugs and backslaps and cheers.

Ryder laughed and his eyes grew misty when he looked into the stands and saw his mother and father on their feet, cheering with the rest of the parents and random spectators just out to enjoy the glory of a perfect spring day. His coach barked them into line. The teams shook hands.

The team huddled up and Coach awarded Ryder the game ball. He'd made several spectacular plays on defense and hit three for four with two home runs. He accepted the smooth round ball, so perfect, and stuffed his gear into the bat bag his father had bought him for his birthday.

He shouldered the bag and turned the ball in his hand as he marched toward the stands, thinking of another baseball from a time that seemed so very long ago. His life was so different now. So wonderful.

His mother hugged him and his father too. Doyle's mustache chaffed his neck and Ryder laughed and pushed him away like he always did. It was a running joke between them, father and son. Ryder took his mother's hand and his eyes focused on the gold band around her finger. He liked to just see it there, as if he were afraid the whole thing hadn't really happened.

But the ring was there, and they really did live in a small two-bedroom apartment on Amsterdam not too far from the firehouse and not too far from Mr. Starr so that they could see him once a week. It was always for dinner, and he and Ryder's dad could go at it about politics and religion and the reasons for the general decline in the world.

"Hey!" Mr. Starr's shout surprised Ryder.

Ryder hadn't seen him during the game and he spun around and said so. Ashleigh Love smiled and said hello, her hands firmly on the back of Mr. Starr's chair.

"That's because I just got here, you knucklehead. More books and less baseball might make you a little sharper between the ears." Mr. Starr didn't look any better than he had a year ago, but he didn't look any worse, and the tone of his voice wasn't quite as sour, despite his determination to be a grouch. "Speaking of books, I've got something for you. I finished it this morning. Well, almost finished it. I still have a couple pages at the end, but I thought you'd like to see it before anyone else. Ashleigh?"

"Oh!" Ashleigh Love dug into the pouch in the back of the chair and removed a thick stack of papers held together by a sturdy metal clip.

Ryder took the manuscript. He read the title page, grinned at Mr. Starr, then at his parents. His mother nodded at the bleachers.

Ryder sat down and flipped Mr. Starr's book open to page one.

*Chapter 1*

*Ryder smashed a ball over the fence and tried not to smile.*
    *He jogged the bases while his teammates whistled, catcalled, or clapped, depending on the kind of person they were and which side they'd bet on. His team's best pitcher, Ben Salisbury, said he'd strike Ryder out with*

*four pitches. Ryder knocked it out on the second. Only the kids who went to Dalton School with Salisbury bet on him, and they did it out of loyalty. Everyone knew Ryder had the best Little League batting average in Manhattan. . . .*

Turn the page for a sneak peek of

# HOME RUN,

the latest in the BASEBALL GREAT
series from Tim Green!

# CHAPTER ONE

**PART OF JOSH LOVED** his father dearly, but another part . . . well, "hate" was a word his mother said you should never use. He did hate some of the things his father *did*. Certainly he hated when his father stood talking to someone, the way he was right now, when he was supposed to be coaching baseball. Thankfully, it was some guy in a suit, not Diane, his dad's girlfriend and the woman who had destroyed their family, huddled up with him in the corner of the dugout. But Josh still stood in the on-deck circle, worried.

Here they were in Baltimore in the championship game of the final tournament of the season, and his dad wasn't even paying attention.

He again pushed the image of Diane from his mind. Instead, he thought of the never-ending stream of representatives from companies like Nike, Legal Sea Foods, and Marucci Sports—who came to Syracuse and scouted the Titans while his dad piled on the charm. He was always trying to get money for the team. That's who Josh had this guy in the suit pegged for, a rep from some sporting goods company.

"Who else wears a suit to a baseball game?" he silently asked himself.

The crack of a bat turned his attention back to the field.

Benji Lido, one of Josh's two best friends in the world, rumbled down the first-base line, scuffing up puffs of white chalk. The ball rebounded off the left-field wall, but a strong-armed outfielder from Oxford, Mississippi, and too many double cheeseburgers under Benji's sizable belt kept him at first. Their pitcher, Kerry Eschelman, was safely on third. Coach Moose, Josh's dad's muscle-bound assistant, was coaching the Titans' runners at third base. He grinned at Esch and pointed toward Josh in the on-deck circle.

Their catcher, Preston McMillan, gave Josh the high sign.

Benji bounced on the first-base bag, clapping his hands and shouting. "This is *it*, y'all. Heavy hitter two is on the bag! Man in scoring position! And heavy hitter one is about to *blast* it over you rebel boys' heads!"

Josh's teammates elbowed each other and snickered. Even Billy Duncan, their tall, awkward right fielder who'd struck out three times already, broke into a grin from his seat on the end of the bench. Jaden Neidermeyer, Josh's other best friend in the world, was in the dugout keeping stats for the team. Jaden buried her face in her hands, covering her striking yellow-green eyes and honey-brown face. The Oxford Wildcats just stared, still amazed at Benji's loudmouth antics even though they'd gotten a full dose of them now for nearly six whole innings.

Josh swung his bat a final time, then stepped out of the on-deck circle heading for the batter's box. The stands behind the backstop teemed with balloons, banners, caps, and colorful summer clothes. Two parents with their fingers curled around the wire of the backstop talked in the loud, rude voices some adults felt free to use in a kid's world.

"Scoring position? Since when is first base scoring position?"

"Since the LeBlanc kid is up next. Everyone on base is in scoring position when that kid hits."

Josh's cheeks warmed, and he directed his gaze ahead at the catcher and umpire, even though he wanted to turn and enjoy the praise from the well-informed strangers. The Titans were down 3–1, but with Benji on first and Kerry Eschelman on third, everyone knew that Josh could win the game—and the entire tournament—with a home run. He'd already hit one in this game, scoring the only run, and he'd hit eight over

3

the course of the last three days.

With two outs under his belt, Josh knew the Wildcats right-hand pitcher would go for the win himself. His name was Kable Milligan, and he had a fastball that seemed magnetically drawn to the low outside corner of the plate. So while players might be able to get a piece of Milligan's pitches, they rarely ever got a solid hit.

Batting left-handed, Josh took a swing at the first pitch and fouled it off. He glanced at the dugout for his father's encouragement, but the guy in the suit still held his attention. Josh knew that if the sports rep was on the fence about awarding the Syracuse Titans travel baseball team some sponsorship, winning this tournament would go a long way toward the right decision. It was all or nothing.

Despite his father's coaching, Josh hated pressure. He knew true champions got cool under pressure, but he could feel the droplets of sweat beading on his upper lip. And when Benji opened his mouth and began to jaw about heavy hitter one, Josh shot him a look and signaled for total silence.

No such luck.

Benji seemed inspired. "That's *right*! Silent but deadly! That's Josh LeBlanc, ladies and gentlemen! That's heavy hitter one! Over and out, good buddy! We're sendin' some whipped Wildcats down the Mississippi on a riverboat *ride*! Ha! Bring me *home*, my fellow heavy hitter!"

Josh shook his head and bit his lip. He stopped looking at Benji, knowing it had been a mistake to try and shush him. Benji and his mouth were two separate things, and while Benji was lovable and funny, his mouth was like a broken toilet. Getting it to stop running was no easy task.

Josh breathed in deeply the smell of dusty dirt and warm grass, hot dogs and cotton candy. He nodded at the ump and locked eyes with the Mississippi pitcher, a lanky, dark-haired kid with freckles and a mean-looking smile. Milligan wound up. In it came, as fast, low, and outside—just as Josh expected.

He stepped toward the plate and barreled up to the ball.

# CHAPTER TWO

*CRACK.*

He could *feel* it. He didn't need to watch.

That ball sailed over the left-field wall.

Josh's team cheered. Benji sashayed around the bases, dancing in front of Josh's slow, steady jog. When Josh crossed home plate and waded through the forest of high fives, he was shocked to see his father hadn't moved from his spot in the corner of the dugout with the stranger. The team was jubilant with a tournament win, but the men were still talking intently.

"Dad?" Josh stood at the entrance to the dugout, looking down and in. Jaden was finishing up the stats. She smiled, giving him a silent thumbs-up for his big home run. But he was unable to return her smile.

"Dad?" he said again. "Is everything okay?"

Josh's father looked up as if waking from a dream. His eyes focused on Josh, and his smile appeared as he nodded his head. "Better than okay, Josh! Nice hit! Great tournament!"

The words suggested everything was fine, but Josh knew his father, his expressions, and his voice well enough to know that something had happened.

In fact, Josh was certain that everything in their lives was about to change.

# CHAPTER THREE

**AS JOSH HEADED TOWARD** his dad, Jaden leaned back to let him pass. She was watching without comment, but her green catlike eyes caught his and froze the moment in time. She had her frizzy hair pulled back in a ponytail. Her straight and narrow nose and the long, dark eyelashes reminded him of the picture in his social studies book of an Egyptian princess.

"Josh?" His father's voice broke the spell. "Come here. There's someone I want you to meet."

His father turned to the stranger. "Josh, this is Jeff Enslinger, the athletic director at Crosby College. . . . It's in Florida. Not far from Orlando."

Mr. Enslinger extended a hand, and Josh took it. "Nice to meet you, Josh."

"Like, Disney World?" It was the only thing that came to Josh's mind.

The AD was nearly as tall as Josh's father but not as thick. He had a weak chin but strong, blue eyes perched above a big, triangular nose. His hair was a blaze of orange spikes. Was he trying to look like a Florida orange?

Mr. Enslinger studied Josh before smiling. "We're about an hour from Disney, but a lot of our students end up working there. There's a whole city underneath that place. You'd be surprised."

"I'd like to go sometime," Josh said.

Mr. Enslinger cleared his throat and gave Josh's dad a questioning look. "Everybody loves Disney."

Josh's dad laughed and thumped Josh's back. "Mr. Enslinger has offered me a job, buddy."

"At Disney?" Josh rumpled his brow.

His father laughed some more, and Mr. Enslinger joined in.

"At Crosby College," his father said. "They've got a Division Three baseball program."

"Which will become Division One in four years," Mr. Enslinger said. "Under your father's direction . . . if he accepts my offer. We're putting a lot of money into it. We've got a deal with Nike to buy all their equipment, and they were the ones who said I should take a look at your dad. He does nothing but win, right?

That's how they described him."

Josh had no idea what to say. Out on the field, the two teams were forming lines to shake hands, baseball players caught up in one of the great traditions of the game. He nodded toward his teammates. "Should we shake hands?"

His father glanced at the field. "For sure! Sorry, Jeff, I'll be right back."

"Of course." Mr. Enslinger gave a short nod suggesting sportsmanship was a welcome quality at Crosby College.

Josh hurried out of the dugout, the joy of the big victory already swallowed up by the tar pit of worry. He looked back and watched his father say something else to Mr. Enslinger, then shake hands before jogging onto the field to join his team. Josh pasted a smile on his face, slapped hands, and mumbled, "Good game good game good game," like some caveman chant as he worked his way through the Wildcats' team roster.

His mind spun with questions, none of them comforting. Where would they live? How would they get down there? What school would he go to? What about his friends? Was there a team he could play for in Florida? Who would coach that team? But most of all Josh worried about his mom. Where did she fit into all this?

And would she even join them?

# CHAPTER FOUR

**JOSH COULDN'T HELP WONDERING** if he might be able to stop the whole thing, alter the course of his and his family's lives that very day. Josh wasn't a kid anymore; he was a young man. That's what his mom called him when she was mad, wasn't it? A young man could make decisions and have an impact on the world around him, right?

It might be possible if he played it right.

Never able to make it to the major leagues, his dad talked all the time about Josh's baseball career. It was as if Josh's life was his father's second chance. A first-round draft pick out of high school, he spent years in the minor and independent leagues before his retirement—forced on him, if Josh was honest. Where his father had failed, Josh would surely succeed. It was at the heart of their relationship. They spent nearly no time together that wasn't on a ball field or at the batting cage, honing his skills. So, if Josh dug his heels in, he just might be able to unravel the whole college thing. . . .

The hint of tears in the corners of the Mississippi pitcher's eyes jarred Josh back into the present moment. Suddenly the slap of hands and the sun blinking down on them both became monumentally important. This game—and this tournament—meant so much to the players in it because each victory was another rung in the ladder toward the majors. That's what his father had taught him. While Benji would jeer if he saw Kable Milligan's tears, Josh felt a bond of brotherhood.

Each star performance gave you a leg up on the other guys. There were thousands—no, hundreds of thousands—of "other" guys. And fewer than four hundred spots in the show for position players like Josh. He knew that from his dad's career. His dad *never* played a game in the majors. He never even got a September call-up to ride the bench and wear a big-league uniform. It was more than tough, so he understood the Mississippi pitcher's feelings immediately. Between the two of them, Josh had won the day . . . and the trophy.